**"I wonder about** [...]
**a low, mesmerizin**[g ...]
**the three tiny ear**[...]

It shouldn't affect her so, she told herself.

"I wonder if Talia took care of her mother when she was sick," he murmured. She nodded slightly, and he stroked her cheek, pausing at the beauty mark near her mouth. "I wonder if Talia took care of Kevin too."

Not trusting her voice, she nodded again.

His finger traced the bow of her upper lip. "I know that Talia takes care of her business, and she takes care of her charity work. But you know what I really wonder?" His face was only inches from hers and her heart pounded in a runaway rhythm.

"What?" she whispered.

He leaned close until their breaths mingled. "I wonder who takes care of Talia."

Automatically, she said, "I don't need—"

His lips landed gently on her open mouth in an extended, leisurely "hello." His firm mouth molded hers, and he learned her pleasure by rubbing his lips against hers, tempting her to respond.

There was a moment when she could have pulled away, but then he deepened the kiss. He led her in a sensual duel, teasing her with lips and tongue until she surrendered. She'd never been lured with such care before. . . .

## WHAT ARE *LOVESWEPT* ROMANCES?

They are stories of true romance and touching emotion. We believe those two very important ingredients are constants in our highly sensual and very believable stories in the *LOVESWEPT* line. Our goal is to give you, the reader, stories of consistently high quality that may sometimes make you laugh, sometimes make you cry, but are always fresh and creative and contain many delightful surprises within their pages.

Most romance fans read an enormous number of books. Those they truly love, they keep. Others may be traded with friends and soon forgotten. We hope that each *LOVESWEPT* romance will be a treasure—a "keeper." We will always try to publish

*LOVE STORIES YOU'LL NEVER FORGET*
*BY AUTHORS YOU'LL ALWAYS REMEMBER*

The Editors

**Loveswept**® 572

# Leanne Banks
## Guardian Angel

BANTAM BOOKS
*NEW YORK · TORONTO · LONDON · SYDNEY · AUCKLAND*

GUARDIAN ANGEL

*A Bantam Book / October 1992*

If you would be interested in receiving protective vinyl
covers for your Loveswept books, please write to this address
for information:

Loveswept
Bantam Books
P.O. Box 985
Hicksville, NY 11802

ISBN 0-553-44286-4

Published simultaneously in the United States and Canada

PRINTED IN THE UNITED STATES OF AMERICA

OPM     0 9 8 7 6 5 4 3 2 1

*This book is dedicated to my sisters, Karen and Janie, for the fights, laughter, tears, and hard-won friendship the years have given us.*

*And special thanks to Bonnie, Carolyn, Janet, and Mary.*

# Prologue

He wasn't a drunk, he was just a little crazy.

At least that was the concensus among the small population of Barringer, Virginia. As twelve-year-old Talia McKenzie frantically pedaled her bike toward home, she saw men push and poke at crazy old Mr. Simmons. Slowing down, she wondered what in the world she should do.

She was an hour past her curfew. Swimming at the lake had been so much fun, though, and her friend, Gina, had brought sandwiches for lunch. Even after Gina had left, Talia had splashed and swum, pretending the August sun wouldn't set. She couldn't pretend away her goose bumps and pruned skin, however, when the water grew cool. And the sun faded in spite of her wishes.

Talia could have stayed at the lake for the rest of her life. An instant jab of guilt squelched that thought, and she sighed. Since her mother had gotten sick in March, it seemed Talia had no time for swimming and pajama parties. She'd spent the entire summer keeping her younger brother, Kevin, out of trouble and caring for her mother.

The only reason Talia had gotten away that day was because her mother's best friend, Opal Taylor, had promised to spend the afternoon with Mama and Kevin.

"Stop it," Mr. Simmons cried in an angry, pitiful voice.

"We'll stop," the taller youth said with an ugly laugh, "when you give us your money."

Talia scowled. Mr. Simmons had very little money and no family. She knew for a fact that the minister let the old man sleep in the church.

Hiding on her bike behind some trees, she looked around in vain for help. Mr. Simmons started yelling louder, and she hoped someone would hear him soon. After all, they stood in a fairly public area, behind the town's movie house.

Not that that was good for Talia. If she didn't get grounded for coming home late, she'd probably get it for taking the shortcut through town. Her mother disapproved of her biking on busy streets, especially at night.

She breathed a sigh of relief when she saw another young man walk toward the trio. He was tall and slim and strode along with a confident gait. The light from a distant streetlamp reflected on his long blond hair and white shirt.

"Hey," she heard him say, "what's the problem?"

The two thugs immediately turned their attention to him. Talia stared at him, too, thinking she couldn't wait to tell Gina about him. He was much more impressive than all those rock stars Gina was always mooning over.

He was a good guy, too, she thought, dividing them up just like in an old western. All he needed was a white hat.

"Nothing we can't handle, rich boy," the tall bully

said. "Mind your own business." He gave the new arrival a hard push.

A lump of fear formed in Talia's throat. What if they carried knives? Mr. Simmons seemed to sense they'd lost interest in him and was edging away. Talia gripped her handlebars tighter. What should she do? Caught up in her anxiety, she didn't hear the ensuing conversation. She did see one of the bad guys punch the rescuer in the stomach.

She winced at the sound of fist against flesh.

Both thugs went after the blond man full force. Still, he held his own with calculated kicks and blows. He didn't seem to give their pounding jabs more than a shrug.

Talia watched in awe. When one of the bullies fell to the ground, it looked as if the rescuer might take them both out.

But the bully staggered to his feet. A cold chill settled over her. She could barely make out the object in his hand, but it looked like a brick.

Something had to be done. Adrenaline rushed through her, and Talia acted on pure instinct. She pedaled furiously toward them. Engrossed with the fighting, the three men didn't see her until it was too late.

She closed her eyes, gritted her teeth, and rode straight into the man holding the brick.

He howled in pain.

Thrown clear from her bike, she began to scream at the top of her lungs. She raised such a furor that several other people rushed to the scene. The teen thugs tried to run away, but a couple of men stopped them.

She heard several appalled murmurs.

"Isn't that Harlan Barringer's son?"

"Trace Barringer?"

"These delinquents will be dead meat when Harlan hears about this."

Another man chuckled. "Looks like Trace took care of them well enough on his own."

Talia just wanted to get away without being recognized. She picked herself up and retrieved her bike. Her knees were skinned. They burned with pain, and she could feel blood running down one leg.

At this rate, she figured she'd be lucky to see the lake again before her fourteenth birthday.

Just as she climbed on her bike, the one they called Trace said, "Hey, wait a minute. You on the bike. I need to thank you."

She gulped as he walked to her. Everyone was staring at her. Acutely aware of her dark, stringy hair and wet clothing, she bit her lip and wished she could make herself disappear.

He gave her a warm smile that made her stomach feel strange, then he offered his hand. Even with his cheek beginning to swell, he was the most attractive man she'd ever seen. She would have liked to see the color of his eyes, but it was too dark.

She rubbed her scraped palm against her shorts before taking his hand. "It was nothing," she whispered, and quickly put her hand back on the handlebar.

"Nothing?" Her heart lifted absurdly at his incredulous tone. "You saved my rear. What are you, some kind of guardian angel?"

She recovered her wits enough to laugh. The last person who'd called her an angel had been her father, right before his death six years earlier. "No angel," she said. "I just evened the odds a little bit." She turned and rode away from the crowd.

# *One*

One of these days, she'd give in to the urge to rip the tinted glasses off his face and see whether his eyes were green or gold.

But not today, Talia McKenzie told herself as she crossed her nylon-clad legs and leaned back in the brown leather chair. Today the only thing she wanted from Trace Barringer was money.

She watched the new ruler of Barringer Corporation as he prowled from one end of his cherry desk to the other, speaking into the phone. A long-fingered hand raked through his blond hair. Actually, it was brown with sparks of blond shot through it. Talia absently pushed a strand of her own dark hair behind her ear and searched Trace's face for signs of stinginess. She hoped he was a generous man.

His dark, baritone voice held just a hint of raspiness. It was the kind of voice that wouldn't need to be raised to command authority. The kind of voice that sensitized all the nerve endings in a woman.

Talia shifted in her chair, then let her gaze follow the line of his navy tailored suit along his well-toned physique. She wondered if the suit was Italian, and smiled. Perhaps it was. But the rest of Trace Barringer was one hundred percent all-American well-bred male.

He'd definitely aged well.

Though he fairly emanated impatience, she noticed he kept it from his tone. Unwillingly, she admired his control.

He concluded his phone conversation and punched another button. "Hold my calls, Dusty." Replacing the receiver, he turned his attention to Talia. "Would you care for coffee or a soft drink?"

"Neither, thank you." She had no desire to make this meeting last one minute longer than necessary.

"Fine." He sat in his chair and studied her for a moment.

His scrutiny unsettled her, and the years fell away, making Talia feel twelve again with skinned knees, stringy hair, and gangly legs. She restrained the urge to smooth her collar or make sure her bra strap wasn't showing. Instead, she twisted a tiny gold earring, thankful she'd chosen to wear two earrings that day instead of her usual six.

He opened a folder. "Ms. McKenzie, according to our records, Barringer Corporation has donated a generous sum of money to the Lung Foundation Drive for the past three years."

"Yes, you have. And it's been greatly appreciated by the Foundation. In the past, I've always dealt with your father. I usually mailed him a letter, then he sent us a check." She'd always wondered if the senior Barringer's donations had been motivated by guilt. "I hope there's no problem with your company giving a donation this year."

Trace shook his head. "No. The company plans to make a donation. But we'd also like to be more involved in the planning of Lung Awareness Month. That's the reason I asked you here today. I'd like to see the drive expanded to the textile mill." He paused and smiled, revealing a slash of strong white teeth.

A lethal weapon, that smile, Talia thought. She wondered how many women had fallen casualty to it.

"In other words," he continued, "we want to be represented on the Planning Committee."

*Over my dead body.* It was one thing to spend fifteen minutes politely requesting a donation from a Barringer. But Talia's mind couldn't conceive of deliberately placing herself in the position of dealing with him or any other Barringer for the three months the fund drive required. "That's really not necessary, Mr. Barringer. At this point, our plans are well under way."

"Please call me Trace. And you're . . . ?"

Ms. McKenzie, she thought peevishly. "Talia," she said with reluctance, and bit her lip. This meeting wasn't going as planned. She'd hoped to be out the door with a hefty check by this time.

His gaze settled on her mouth. "Talia." He tried it out, as if he were tasting a new wine. She waited, shifting uncomfortably when his intent gaze trailed down to her crossed legs.

The intercom buzzed. He snatched up the phone. "Dusty, I told you—" He paused, and his entire demeanor changed. His eyebrows drew together while he muttered a curse. "I'll take it. Tell Madelyn to hold on for one minute."

Punching the hold button, he turned back to Talia. "We won't be able to get anything settled here. Can I meet you for dinner tonight?"

Dinner! Shock ran through her until she found her voice. "Uh, no. I already have plans."

He checked his calendar. "How about tomorrow night?"

"I don't think so." How did one politely say "When hell freezes over?" she wondered.

"Next Monday?"

"No."

He cocked his head and studied her for a moment. "How about if you tell me what evening you have available?"

She lifted her shoulders. "My mind draws a complete blank." At least that was the truth. She hadn't been able to think straight since he'd suggested dinner. She shook her head and stood. "I'm sorry. I'll send you our tentative plans and budget. Then you can decide what kind of donation Barringer Corporation will be able to make."

He opened his mouth to speak as she left, but the buzzer sounded again. She'd lay odds that he was rarely thwarted. When she saw the look of frustration on his face, she almost felt sorry for him.

Almost.

"Thank you, Mr. Barringer," she murmured, and closed the door behind her.

A curious combination of relief and disappointment bubbled within her as she left the building. He hadn't recognized her.

Ten minutes later Talia swept into her deli, On A Roll. "Thanks for watching the store for me, Gina." She strapped a red apron over her white blouse and navy linen skirt as her very pregnant friend waddled out from behind the counter.

"How'd it go?" Gina asked. "No, don't tell me. I want to hear everything from start to finish, and right now I've got to get home to meet Jason at the bus stop."

Accustomed to the way Gina tended to carry on a

conversation with herself, Talia just smiled and put some cookies in a bag. "Take these with you. And about Jason, can I borrow him one evening while you and Don go out to dinner?"

Gina narrowed her blue eyes at Talia. "I've got your number. You know I won't accept money for helping you, but I'd never turn down free babysitting." She gave Talia's shoulder a squeeze before she opened the door. "I'll call you tonight. And I want every juicy detail about Trace Barringer. Don tells me all the women at the plant swoon when he comes around."

Fortunately, the door swung shut before Talia could reply. She waved good-bye through the window, then reached for her tape of *Carmen*. Flipping it into her tape player, she sighed as the music washed over her. She saved *Carmen* for her most depressing or disturbing days. D-days, she called them.

And today had been most disturbing.

She didn't want to think about the source of her disturbing feelings. If she examined the source, then she'd remember the blond male lead in a thousand of her adolescent daydreams.

She'd always carried a crazy image of Trace Barringer as her knight in shining armor. The image had brought her comfort during the years of her mother's illness. Times when Talia had felt like weeping. Times when she could have used a strong shoulder to share the load.

Trace's appeal had only increased with age. He emanated the kind of confidence a man gained from repeatedly proving himself in challenging situations. Considering that she may have unwittingly presented him with a challenge, Talia felt a vague shiver of premonition and turned away from her unsettling thoughts.

Out of habit, she checked the small dining area of

her shop. Everything was clean. She should have known Gina would keep the shop immaculate. Though most of her business was take-out, a few customers enjoyed eating at the wooden bar that served as a windowsill, or at one of the four round tables. Owning the solitary sub shop in small-town Barringer had its advantages. The absence of competitors allowed her to enjoy her brisk business without constantly looking over her shoulder.

On A Roll brought her a great deal of pride and pleasure. She'd worked hard for it. So had her brother, Kevin, in spite of his hurt and confusion over their mother's death. In spite of what the Barringers had done to him. Her blood seethed just thinking about it, and she wondered how Trace could ooze integrity when his family was a bunch of vipers.


"Another donation to my ex-wife's favorite charity—herself," Trace muttered as he signed the check.

At least he knew it wouldn't be long before Madelyn's acting career took off. If ever a woman belonged on stage, it was she. Madelyn was the kind of woman who never got off the stage. She wasn't honest. She wasn't real.

An image of the intriguing lady who'd raced out of his office minutes before hovered in his mind. Talia McKenzie. Now *she* was real. She may have wanted to conceal her emotions, but her feelings showed in every move she made. A nervous self-conscious twisting of a tiny earring. A flash of fire in her dark eyes.

And she'd bit into her generous lower lip with small white teeth. Trace pulled off his glasses and wondered what had been going on in her mind.

She was a little hostile. A little challenging.

And a whole lot of temptation.

Leaning back in his leather chair, he tried to remember the last time a woman had really tempted him. He couldn't.

He'd spent too many years trying to fix a marriage that had started out broken. He'd spent too many months trying to gain custody of his young son without an ugly court battle. And the family company had demanded every spare minute since his father's heart attack the previous year.

He glanced at the signed check in front of him. It was only a matter of time before Madelyn gave him custody of Robby. She was weakening. She knew her life wasn't stable enough for an active four-year-old. It was only a matter of time.

Perhaps he'd put his personal life and needs on hold long enough. Trace felt a very masculine stirring when he recalled the challenging sparkle in Talia's eyes.

He savored it and grinned.

When he punched the button for his secretary, she picked up immediately. "Yes, Mr. Barringer?"

"Dusty, you should be receiving some correspondence concerning Lung Awareness Month from Talia McKenzie. Bring it to my attention when you get it."

"You don't want Public Relations handling this?" She sounded surprised.

That would be the practical thing to do. Barringer Corporation had a PR department for this kind of thing. And he really didn't have time. Trace didn't hesitate. "No, I'll handle this myself."

One week later Talia set the oven on preheat to bake the brownies she'd just mixed. The lights dimmed. "Oh, great," she muttered, then watched with resigned futility as the lights went out in her small Cape Cod. Daylight Saving Time didn't kick in until next week, so the house was covered in a veil of darkness. Turning, she groped through the kitchen drawer that held extra fuses.

Was that a knock at the front door? "Give me just a minute," she called. It was probably one of the members of the Planning Committee arriving for their scheduled meeting that night.

She felt an assortment of pens, rubber cement, paper clips, and coupons, but no fuses. Muttering to herself, she headed for her bedroom. She kept a few in her nightstand for emergencies.

Someone pounded on her front door again. "Hold your horses," she yelled. It was probably Lou Adkins, the printer. The guy couldn't stand waiting. Reaching into the bottom drawer of the nightstand, she stretched her fingers to the back and found a fuse. "Thank you, Lord."

"Having problems?" a deep voice said behind her. It wasn't Lou.

Talia whirled around and just barely swallowed back the scream in her throat. A squeak came out in its place. Her heart beat wildly; her knees all but knocked together.

She stepped backward. "Who are you? What are you doing here?"

The man walked toward her and she gulped. Where was her flashlight? She could tell by his shadow that he was quite tall and broad-shouldered.

Strange how the brain functioned in moments of crisis. Her mind raced a million miles in a few seconds as she considered what man would enter her bedroom.

The only man who'd overtly attempted to woo her

lately was Mick Ramsey from the auto parts store. The last time he'd come in for lunch, he had reeked of garlic. Upon his departure, he'd informed her, with nauseating suggestiveness, that the Chinese considered garlic an aphrodisiac. Talia figured he'd retrieved that scintillating bit of information purely by accident. Mick wasn't the type to stretch his reading past the sports page or the back of a cereal box.

She sniffed suspiciously, but the faint scent she caught was an intriguing blend of woodsy aftershave and man. "Mick?"

The intruder reached for something on her night-stand. "No. But if that's who you were expecting, I can pretend to change my name." Amusement wove its way through his dark voice. "It's Trace. Trace Barringer." He turned on her flashlight. "Is this what you were looking for?"

Blinking, Talia reached for the flashlight and tried not to dwell on how her pulse had picked up when she'd heard his name. "Yes. How did you get in?"

"Your door was unlocked. I saw the lights go out and thought you might need some help."

"Oh," she mumbled, resolving to lock her door in the future. "The wiring in this house is ancient," she said nervously as she made her way into the hall to turn off the air conditioner. "If I use the air condi-tioner and the oven at the same time, it often blows the fuse for the ground level of the house."

"So replace the wiring," Trace suggested.

"There's this small matter of college tuition for my brother," she answered before realizing that Trace Barringer wouldn't understand the concept of hav-ing to choose carefully how to spend one's money. She felt him prowling along behind her and tried to shove aside her discomfort at having him in her house. It would be easier to ignore a lion following her.

"Why are you here?" she asked.

"For the planning meeting. There was a list of the meeting times on the memo Ms. Taylor sent me. With your *busy* schedule, this seemed the only way to meet with you."

Darn. Talia had been so eager to be rid of anything relating to Trace Barringer, she'd asked another committee member to keep him informed. If Talia had sent him the information, she would have been careful to omit the meeting times.

Distracted by her thoughts, she stumbled over the edge of the hall carpet and pitched forward. "Oh!" Her knees hit the floor and pain shot through her legs. Before she had time to throw out her hands, Trace wrapped an arm around her waist and drew her up.

"Hey, what happened?" His voice was edged with husky concern.

Talia's breath caught in her throat. She didn't know which was worse, the pain in her knees or the sensation of Trace's hard body pressed against her back. "I tripped over the carpet," she finally said.

"Are you hurt?"

"Just my knees."

"Let me see. Sit down." He released her and retrieved the flashlight that had flown out of her hand.

"No. It's not that bad, and it's dark," she protested. She was uncomfortable with the darkness and his nearness. She also wished she hadn't given in to a fit of spring fever earlier and put on shorts.

He grabbed her hand and gave a gentle but firm tug. "I can use the flashlight. Come on."

He joined her on the floor and began to examine her knees with his hands. It was strange, sitting in the middle of her hall with Trace's hands on her bare legs. She couldn't see his face clearly. He used such a gentle touch, she could almost forget he was a Barringer.

One of his fingers grazed the inside of her thigh. She gasped at the provocative thrill that ran through her.

He stopped, then touched her the same way again. "Does this hurt?"

"N-no. I guess my legs are just sensitive," she said, honestly.

The following silence hung thickly between them, and a weird tension zinged through the air. She wondered if he felt it too. It was only the darkness, she told herself.

Pulling her leg away she scrambled to her feet, damning the sound of her quickened breathing.

Trace followed, his large frame looming over hers. "Are you okay?"

"Fine. I just got a little shook up. The fall," she added quickly, and turned away.

Back in the kitchen, she concentrated on replacing the blown fuse. She was glad to have something to do with her hands. Instantly the lights came on. "Voilà," she said, smiling and extending her arms dramatically.

"Incredible," Trace murmured. What had happened, he wondered, to the French twist, conservative suit, and pursed lips of the disapproving woman who'd been in his office? At least, he thought, the legs were the same, long, shapely, silky, the kind of legs that led men to dream wild fantasies. Her hair was a mass of tempestuous waves, and her brown eyes sparkled with fire. And her lips . . . His mouth went dry at the sight of her rosy lips.

He looked back at her eyes and held her gaze for

several seconds until she looked away. Shy, he concluded, until she spared him another glance. With surprise, he noted the banked hostility in her eyes.

She turned and bent, placing the brownies in the oven. It took enormous control, but he unglued his gaze from her tempting rear end. Feeling the heat for the first time that evening, he tugged at his collar and studied the daisy-print wallpaper.

"Mr. Barringer, do you have some questions about the plans we've made for Lung Awareness Month?" Talia asked as she turned on the coffeemaker.

"Trace," he corrected her. "I have a few. But they can be answered during the meeting. I'm actually more curious about you."

Her polite smile didn't reach her eyes. He found himself longing for the alluring smile she'd given him just moments before.

"As I told you before, Mr. Barringer, I appreciate your interest in LAM, but the Planning Committee is already formed. I'll be happy to keep you informed. However, your presence isn't really . . . " Her voice drifted off, and she bit her lip.

She'd done that in his office, and he wondered if she knew how sensual the gesture was. He sensed something familiar about her, but couldn't put a label on it. Shoving a hand in his pocket, he stepped closer. She took a step back. "You're saying my presence isn't necessary," he said in a low, challenging voice.

She raised her chin. "I have to believe the CEO of Barringer Corporation has better ways to spend his time than as a member of a Planning Committee for LAM. Wouldn't it be more convenient if you just had your secretary send me your ideas?"

"Perhaps," he conceded. "But convenience isn't

always the primary consideration. I would think you'd be happy to extend your influence directly to the textile mill."

A hint of vulnerability filtered into her gaze. She looked away.

"Tell me, Talia," he asked gently. "How did you get involved with this project?"

"My mother died of pneumonia several years ago." She paused. "She also had emphysema. The doctor said she was weak, that she worked too hard."

Trace nodded. So that was it. "She worked at the mill."

"Yes."

"And you blame the mill."

"No."

She said it too quickly, and her self-deprecating smile showed she knew he'd seen through her denial. "In the beginning I blamed the mill," she confessed. "I was very angry. My mother had to work so hard after my father died. But she was the kind of person who would have worked hard no matter where she was employed. Her supervisor was always very understanding about her illness." Talia sighed. "Sometimes I thought if she hadn't had Kevin and me, she would have been much better off."

Trace recognized guilt when he saw it and felt some of her sadness. "You don't really believe she would have been happier without you?"

Talia shook her head, her hair tumbling around her shoulders in a silky curtain. "No. Angelina McKenzie loved her babies more than anything. But I was just nineteen years old. All of a sudden I was responsible for raising my fifteen-year-old brother." She closed her eyes against the remembered pain. "Her death was horrible. But the year after was . . ." She stopped, unable to find the words to describe it.

Trace stepped forward, wanting to comfort her in some way. To touch her hand or shoulder. To offer words that would soothe her wounds. It was an unusual feeling for him. Since he'd become CEO for Barringer Corporation, he'd had little time for tenderness. For that matter, in the last few years his emotional life had become a barren wasteland.

Her sad brown eyes proved his undoing. He couldn't find the words, so he took her small hand in his and lifted it to his lips.

Her eyes widened at the gesture. She pulled back, but he held firm. He kissed her hand and found himself wanting to extend the gentle caress to her lips. For one long moment they stared into each other's eyes, then he tugged at her hand, wanting her closer.

# *Two*

Someone knocked on the front door.

Talia jerked back, looking as if she'd touched a snake. "That must be the committee members. I'll let them in."

Trace watched her bolt from the kitchen, his eyes narrowed thoughtfully. A man could incur some heavy losses under that kind of woman's influence, he decided. Loss of perspective. Loss of sleep. Loss of sanity.

His body was still tense with the excitement of merely being close to her, kissing her hand and touching her silky legs. He remembered how her eyes had grown soft and vulnerable. Odd, he mused. It was almost as if she'd forgotten who he was.

Then she'd turned to ice.

Talia swung open the door and greeted the committee members as if they were the cavalry coming to her rescue. Accompanied by the two middle-aged men and one woman, she walked back into the kitchen and made the introductions. Lou Adkins, Opal Taylor, and Darryl Harris, one of the vice presidents at the local bank.

Since the three arrivals wore expressions varying from surprise to distrust, Talia supposed Trace would have his hands full winning them over. It would be interesting to watch. And she was relieved to have his attention directed away from herself.

"I'm going to check on the brownies," she said. "You can go into the den."

After the others left, she set the brownies on the counter to cool, poured the coffee, and set the cups on a tray. Untenable though it may be, she knew she was drawn to Trace. But, as easily as she accepted her curiosity about him, she knew she wouldn't do a thing about it.

She picked up the tray. Her shaking hands caused the cups to clatter noisily, and she uttered a mild curse. How was she supposed to be calm and collected with Trace Barringer in her house?

She didn't want his attention, she reminded herself as she walked into the living room. She wanted his donation.

The meeting progressed as the group mapped out more plans for Lung Awareness Month. Though she tried to concentrate on each word, Talia found her gaze repeatedly drawn to Trace. Although he sat relaxed and quiet, she'd bet he could recite every detail of the discussion.

Watching his deliberate examination of her living room, she wondered what conclusions he was making. What did he think of the oak end tables her father had made before he died? The homey green sofa and slightly lumpy chairs? Did he recognize Kevin from the picture on the wall? Could he possibly know the porcelain bunny collection on the second shelf of the bookcase was one of her weaknesses? And why did she feel he'd gained too much knowledge of her just from his perusal of the room?

His gaze slid from the bunnies to her eyes, and she wondered, inanely, if he could read her mind. Then he was studying the little mole above the right corner of her mouth. She had to purse her lips to resist the urge to run her tongue over the mark.

Flustered by his quiet, invasive attention, she forced her eyes away from him.

When Trace finally spoke, he offered his opinions and suggestions with utter politeness. "Since you have a dual goal of raising both awareness and funds, it sounds as if you've got a good start. I'd like some posters for the mill, Lou, if you could manage that." Lou nodded, and Trace continued without missing a beat. "The mill could sponsor an event. Perhaps a bowling tournament or a night at the roller skating rink. And I think you could increase your donations significantly if you generated some interest from the country club."

They all stared at him. That last suggestion had the impact of a small bomb, because none were members of the country club.

The silence was unnerving. Knowing she would have squirmed under such intense scrutiny, Talia gave him points for sitting in her lumpy chair with a confident, expectant expression on his face.

Opal Taylor cleared her throat. Darryl Harris pushed his glasses back on his nose. Lou Adkins studied his fingernails. The only sound in the room was the ticking of her mother's anniversary clock.

Talia sighed. Since she would receive no help from her fellow committee members, she'd better go ahead and respond. "I think your suggestions are very helpful. Getting the mill involved would increase awareness among the part of the population who need the information."

She paused and chose her next words carefully.

"As far as the country club is concerned, you already have connections with the members there. It seems logical that you would be the one to represent our committee." There, she thought. That hadn't been so bad.

Trace hooked an ankle over the opposite knee and smiled. "I'll be glad to represent the committee." He pulled an appointment book from his suit coat, which he'd hung over the side of the chair. "However, since I've only just become involved in this project, I'd like another committee member to come along with me. Talia, are you available Saturday night? We could meet a few of the club's charter members for dinner."

"Not in a million years," she said under her breath.

He raised an eyebrow. "Excuse me?"

Talia couldn't bear that penetrating gaze one more minute. She felt as if he'd been studying her the entire evening. If that wasn't galling enough, she'd had a hard time tearing her own attention away from him!

She stood and collected the coffee cups and dessert plates. "Actually, I was wondering if one of the other members would be interested in helping you out. I'm pretty busy. What do you think, Opal?" She sent her late mother's best friend her most persuasive look. "You'd probably enjoy an evening out."

Opal gave a self-conscious little giggle. "I don't have anything appropriate to wear for a night out at the country club, Talia dear. Besides," she continued coyly, "Mr. Barringer is such a young, attractive man. He needs a young, attractive escort."

Talia barely stifled her groan. Trace had won Opal over, but Talia hadn't lost yet. "Well, what about you, Darryl? Perhaps you could bring your wife with you."

Darryl again nervously arranged his glasses on his thin nose. "Nancy and I have a standing date for dinner at her mother's house on Saturday nights." His voice held a note of apology. "They're both pretty insistent about it."

"Oh, but for just one night—" Talia broke off when she saw Darryl's strained expression. She was beginning to feel desperate.

With her brightest smile, she turned to her last, most futile hope, and tried to ignore the amused light in Trace's eyes. "Lou, I'll bet you haven't—"

"I've got poker Saturday night," he said bluntly.

If she didn't get out of that room, Talia knew she was going to scream. She picked up the tray of cups and saucers and carried it into the kitchen. Once there, she resisted the urge to test the dish manufacturer's warranty against breakage by flinging a few pieces against the wall.

Instead, she took a deep breath and counted to ten.

Squaring her shoulders, she marched back into the living room where the group waited expectantly. Just as she opened her mouth to refuse, Trace said, "Talia, we can set this up for another time if Saturday night is inconvenient."

He sounded so reasonable. "Of course," he continued in a bland tone, "it would be a shame to give up all those potential donations."

With that, he nailed her coffin shut. If Talia turned down this opportunity, she'd be doing a disservice to the agency that had appointed her, the people who were depending on her, and, in a way, to her mother's memory. She forced the words from her mouth. "What time shall I meet you?"

Wearing an indiscernible expression, Trace stood

and pulled on his suit coat. "That won't be necessary. I'll pick you up."

"No, thank you."

He stopped in the midst of straightening his tie and studied her. "I insist."

"No." She abandoned any attempt at tact. He wanted to bulldoze her. She could see it in his eyes. But he was too clever to push her any further tonight.

"Six o'clock in the lounge," he said, and walked to the front door.

Within three minutes they were all gone. Sensing her mood, the other committee members patted her shoulder on their way out. Opal touched Talia's cheek and murmured, "You go on and have a good time." Too weary to take Opal to task, Talia merely thanked the older woman for coming.

When her home was quiet and empty again, she leaned against the door and closed her eyes. Even though Trace was gone, the air still hummed with tension. She could smell his woodsy aftershave, see his wicked smile.

Moaning at her predicament, she thought of her brother. He would die if he knew she was going out with Trace Barringer, even for charity's sake. She could imagine the betrayal he would feel.

They both bore a grudge against the Barringers, and her Sicilian blood ran hot when she remembered what they'd done to her only brother. She unapologetically, unequivocally detested them.

If one good thing had come out of the evening, it was that she would never again have to restrain herself from pulling off Trace's glasses to determine his eye color. She'd waited fourteen years to find out, and he had stood close enough for her to see that they were a penetrating green.

• • •

After a restless night, Talia was woken by the insistent ringing of her phone. She rolled over and blindly reached toward the noise coming from her nightstand.

"Hello," she murmured in a sleep-husky voice.

"Talia, this is Trace Barringer. Did I wake you?"

"Oh, no," she said automatically, and wondered if everyone lied about being asleep when the phone rang.

"Right," he said. His low chuckle brought her nerve endings pleasantly to life. "I wouldn't have called this early, but I think I left my wallet at your house."

Talia's eyes flew open.

"Would you mind," he went on, "if I pick it up on my way into the office? I can be at your front door in about twenty minutes."

Her mind was still stuck on the wallet as she absently repeated, "Twenty minutes."

"Right. I'll see you then."

*Click.*

"Wait!"

She sat up abruptly, then pounded her fist against the mattress in frustration. Like a punch-drunk fighter, she shook her head to clear it. She was never at her finest in the morning. "Trace Barringer is going to be here in twenty"—she glanced at the clock—"in nineteen minutes *for his wallet.*"

In her panicked mind, she saw an eerie similarity between this incident and the one that had happened years ago between Philip Barringer and her brother. When Philip had invited Kevin to the Barringer estate for a night of pool and pizza, Kevin had practically leaped at the opportunity.

After all, Philip had made it plain that he didn't want Kevin dating his sister, Valerie. With the invitation, Kevin had assumed Philip had changed his mind, that he now found Kevin acceptable.

It had all been a dirty trick.

Kevin had left the Barringers' home with a false sense of hope and some family jewelry planted in his car by Philip. He hadn't even made it all the way home before the sheriff stopped him.

Talia wondered if the practice of framing people ran in the Barringer family. Should she expect the police to show up with Trace?

She glanced at the clock again. Fifteen minutes. There was a reasonable explanation for this, she told herself, but part of her wondered if this was Trace's idea of a sick joke.

Fourteen minutes.

With her heart thundering in her chest, she tossed the covers aside and raced to the shower.

Her hair was wet, but she was clean, alert, and wearing decent clothing when she answered his knock. She thrust the eelskin wallet at Trace as if it were a grenade.

"Here it is. It was hidden under the cushions. I practically tore the chair apart, but nothing seemed to have slipped out. You might—" She broke off her verbal sprint when she noticed the strange way he was studying her.

Dressed in a chalk-striped suit, he stood with one hand resting on his hip. It was a very masculine, very powerful stance. A tingle of awareness ran through her. Having Trace Barringer's undivided attention was pretty heady stuff.

She cleared her throat. "You might want to make sure everything is there." She looked at his wallet and waited expectantly.

He shrugged and put the wallet away. "I'm not really worried about it. I just realized I'd left it here last night and I never know when I'll get called out of town. Between your schedule and mine . . . " His voice trailed off, and he gave her a grin that had nothing to do with schedules.

She tried to ignore the quick flutter of her heart. "I'd really feel better if you looked through it now." When he wrinkled his brow, she explained, "Since you misplaced it at my house, it would set my mind at ease if you made sure everything's in the right place."

He paused, then took the wallet back out and riffled through the credit cards and money. "It looks okay to me. But I would have been very upset to find this missing." He flipped to a photograph and showed it to her.

Feeling foolish for overreacting, she let out a long breath of relief. The man had simply left his wallet by accident and she'd had a full-scale anxiety attack over it. She smiled weakly and looked at the photograph. A pint-sized version of Trace looked back at her. "Your son?"

He nodded. "You see the family resemblance?"

She studied the towheaded charmer with the heartbreaker smile. "How could I miss? He's adorable. He's got your smile."

"Thank you. I'll assume that means you think I'm adorable." Trace chuckled at the disconcerted expression on her face. She'd appeared so panicked when she first opened the door, and he was glad she seemed more relaxed. Her hair was starting to dry into tousled waves that reminded him of rich silk.

He'd love to put his hands through it.

Her clothing was perfectly respectable, yet he

couldn't help but wonder if she wore a bra beneath the aqua T-shirt.

"You assume quite a bit, Mr. Barringer."

He tore his gaze from her shirt up to her beautiful eyes. "Talia," he said in mock offense. "I'm beginning to think you have something against me. And I know that can't be true, because you don't know me yet."

He said the last phrase like a promise, Talia thought, as though she was going to get to know him if he had anything to do with it. Biting her tongue didn't keep her retort back this time.

"You're smarter than I thought, Mr. Barringer."

He laughed, and she hated him for having a sense of humor. Most men in his position would be pompous. He was entirely too charming for her good. Furthermore, he made her want things she couldn't have. She backed away and turned the doorknob behind her. "If you'll excuse me, I need to finish getting ready for work."

She'd just about made it through the door when he clasped her hand and lifted it to within an inch of his lips. Talia's heart lodged in her throat.

"Saturday night, Talia. And my name is Trace." His gaze held hers as he deliberately turned her hand over and pressed his warm mouth against the racing pulse in her wrist. The effect was like liquid flame racing through her bloodstream.

When he loosened his grip, she snatched her hand back, resisting the urge to rub away the effect of his light caress. "Saturday night," she whispered, and miraculously managed to back her way through the door without falling.

She watched him walk away with that same confident stride he'd had fourteen years ago. He walked like a man who knew how to get what he wanted.

• • •

"Just a minute please, Freddie," Talia said as she pulled a food order from her fax machine. After noting the number and types of subs ordered, she mentally calculated how long it would take to fill the order.

"Is that *Aida* you're playing today, Talia?" Freddie asked.

She turned and smiled at the shy young man. She had a soft spot for Freddie, probably because he was the same age as her brother. "Yes, it is. You've been listening to Verdi more."

Her smile faltered when she saw a man walk up behind Freddie. Trace. Her heartbeat quickened.

"What can I get for you today?" she asked, focusing on Freddie again. She tried not to think about the attractive blond man who'd never set foot in her deli before that day. A difficult task, considering the way he was studying her.

"I'll take a meatball sub and a cola," Freddie said. "How's your fax machine working out? Sometimes I think we use it more than the telephone or mail."

"It's been great. Kevin nagged me to get it, you know, and I love it. This way I don't have to answer the phone as much. Especially for large orders." Large orders from the Barringer complex. What was Trace doing there? She had deliveries taken over to the main offices every day at lunch.

Freddie grinned. "I know all about those large orders. The secretaries usually ask me to tally up an order and send it to you. I guess they figure since I'm a messenger for the Barringer complex, it's easy enough for me to take orders for lunch when I deliver memos and the mail."

Growing weary of the Barringer name, Talia just smiled and rang up Freddie's sub and soda.

"If you ever need any help with that fax machine," Freddie said as he took his order from her, "you let me know. I do a lot of—" He was so intent on watching Talia that he backed right into Trace.

"Oh! Excuse me." Freddie's pudgy cheeks flooded with color. "Mr. Barringer," he gasped.

Talia thought she heard a faint "Oh my God" too. Her heart went out to Freddie as he struggled with both his words and his wide plaid tie.

She gazed beseechingly at Trace.

He put a steadying hand on the younger man's shoulder. "That's no problem, Freddie. I probably shouldn't have been standing so close." He shared a "we men have to stick together" grin with Freddie and lowered his voice. "Besides, she's pretty distracting."

If possible, Freddie's face turned brighter red. He mumbled something unintelligible, then ran out the door.

Talia expelled a disgusted sigh. "Well, I'll know not to look to you for help in the future."

"I was just trying to put him at ease. It's obvious he's got a crush on you."

"He does not!"

"Are you kidding? The poor guy couldn't tear his eyes from your shirt the whole time he was in here. And I don't think he's that enamored with the logo on it."

"Right. And Dolly Parton's my twin sister." Well acquainted with the assets and deficits of her lean body, Talia had faced the fact long ago that *Playboy* wouldn't be beating down her door with offers. Still, Trace's remarks left her feeling unsettled. And the fact that his gaze remained on her logo didn't exactly help matters.

She turned away and picked up the order from the fax machine. "Was there something else, Mr. Barringer? I don't have time to chat right now." That wasn't exactly true. The lunch crowd had cleared out a few minutes before.

The impersonal way she said his last name annoyed Trace. He wanted to hear his first name from her lips. He wanted to watch her tempting mouth form the word. Talia had something against him and he had no earthly idea what it was.

He considered using the straightforward approach of asking her flat out, but she was acting too cool. He found he liked her better a little off balance.

A kiss would do the trick. She'd either go off like a firecracker or melt in his arms. Or, he thought with a touch of irony, she'd pick up one of those sharp knives from the counter and use it on him.

An outrageous idea formed in his mind, and he grinned wickedly. Slipping behind the counter while she turned her back to him, he moved close enough to her to feel the warmth from her body.

"Trace," he said into her ear.

Talia spun around, startled to find him so near. That was why she was dizzy, she told herself. Not because of his tantalizing scent. Not because of his inviting green eyes. And certainly not because of the naturally seductive timbre of his voice.

"Dolly Parton's okay," he went on, "but you're more my style—sleek and firm."

The intimate remark embarrassed her, though it was nice to know he approved of her body. She cleared her throat and started to speak, but he continued in a low, matter-of-fact voice.

"Yep," he said, "you're just right. Not too firm, soft

enough to mold to a man's hand. And I bet you're responsive. It would probably only take a couple of flicks from my thumb."

The room grew very warm. Her shirt felt tight, her breasts heavy. He stood too close, yet he was careful not to touch her. Talia swallowed hard. "You should—"

"I imagine you taste sweet, like honey or cream." He kept on as if she hadn't spoken.

His words paralyzed her vocal cords. She knew she should be appalled, but she was oddly mesmerized by his fantasies. The sub shop faded away as the picture of him with his mouth on her breast formed in her mind. She bit back a moan as her nipples pushed against the cotton of her shirt.

"I'd want to feel you against my chest," he whispered. "You know, there's something about a woman's soft naked breasts rubbing against a man's hard, bare chest that drives a man crazy."

Images raced on through her mind like a movie, each more erotic than the last. Trace's muscular chest, her pouting breasts, rubbing, caressing each other. Though she'd never seen his chest before, she could feel it in her hands, hard and muscular with crinkly hair. Her breath came in short spurts. Her knees turned to liquid.

He leaned toward her, his eyes intent on her face. She could feel his arousal, but it brought her no comfort to know his verbal torture had done him in too. He'd drummed up a fever within her, and all her secret places throbbed with life. In some distant, coherent corner of her mind she knew she should push him away.

His chest grazed her aching breasts. She didn't bother to withhold the moan this time. "Talia, haven't you heard that more than a mouth—"

"Stop," she choked out, and covered his mouth with her hand. Shaking her head, she whispered, "We're in the middle of a deli. For Pete's sake, what do you want from me?"

He considered that. "We don't have time for me to answer that question completely." He took hold of her hand and kissed it. "Besides, you're not ready. And I never rush."

He dropped her singed hand and stepped away. "I've already had lunch. I dropped by to tell you we won't be meeting with the country club members on Saturday night."

Talia felt as though he were changing her gears without using the clutch. She tried desperately to keep up. The country club. He'd said something about the country club.

"Saturday night?" she asked.

"Yes." He seemed pleased with her bemusement. "I had to change it to next Saturday, since I have to go out of town. Is next week okay with you?"

"I don't know. Perhaps one of the other committee members might—"

"Come on, Talia, we've been through this before. No one else will do it."

Totally confused by his nonchalant attitude, she turned away from him and began slicing sub rolls with short, jerky movements. "Well, maybe I don't want to go. Maybe I don't trust you after the way you, you . . . " She broke off in frustration.

"After I what?" he asked far too innocently.

She counted to ten. She was hot: angry hot and aroused hot. "After the way you talked to me."

"Did I say something threatening? Was I insulting?" He sidled close to her again, and she felt the space around her shrink. "I was just telling the truth. You can't fault a man for that. As a matter of fact, you have all the more reason to trust me if I tell the truth."

Her head started to pound. "Are you sure you're not a lawyer?"

He smiled sympathetically. "I have a law degree, but I'm not practicing now that I'm CEO."

*Not practicing?* she repeated silently. *You could have fooled me.* She wanted him out of her shop so she could regain her equilibrium. Giving in now seemed the lesser of two evils. "What time next Saturday night?"

"Same time. Six o'clock in the lounge. We'll be having dinner with the two Misses Fitzgerald."

She nodded. "I'll be there." She turned to watch as he strode to the door.

Just before he left, he said, "By the way, you've got a great logo."

Talia spent the better part of the next week wondering what had possessed her to allow Trace to speak to her in such an intimate manner. For that matter, what had possessed *him* to speak to her that way? When her mind could provide no suitable answer, she threw her arms up in frustration and vowed to think of anything but Trace Barringer.

If her heart raced at the thought of him, she ignored it. If the image of his heated gaze taunted her day and night, she pushed it aside. But in her deepest, darkest fantasies, she remembered his graphic analysis of her breasts and paid him back in spades.

During a day trip to Richmond, she splurged on a new dress and French perfume. She chose a soft white frock with a shawl collar and V neck. It skimmed over her slim curves with womanly appeal down to a knee-length pleated hem that flirted against her long legs.

When she asked the saleswoman the translation for the name of the perfume, the older woman got a naughty gleam in her eye. She drew out the three syllable word with a flourish. "Ecstasy."

Dismayed, Talia was thankful her natural tan concealed blushes. Otherwise, her cheeks would have been flaming red. She consoled herself with the knowledge that she could keep that information to herself. Besides, she preferred to smell like something besides salami and meatballs.

Before she felt sufficiently prepared for enduring a dinner with Trace at the country club, it was Saturday evening. Her new clothes did give her a measure of confidence, and the perfume made her feel sensual and feminine. Still, when she pictured the two women she was supposed to meet that night, her stomach fluttered with nervousness.

Talia envisioned a pair of eagle-eyed society matrons who would assess every thread of her clothing, every piece of faux jewelry, and every hair on her head. In an act of defiance, she wore her hair down.

She'd chewed off her rose lipstick for the second time when the phone rang. Her stomach fluttered again. Could it be Trace?

"Hey, Little Italy," a man said when she answered. "How's life in the fast lane?"

Talia smiled. That nickname had been a source of torment throughout her elementary school years. The only person she allowed to call her that was Kevin. "You're walking on thin ice, *baby* brother. You know how I feel about my name. Since exam week is coming up soon, I'll assume your anxieties have rendered you temporarily insane. I'll excuse you this time. And I've noticed you only call me Italia when you're more than an arm's reach away."

Kevin laughed. "Yeah, well, I like my face the way it is."

"As do all the women in Massachusetts." She checked her watch. "So, why are you calling me on a Saturday night?"

She could picture his broad-shouldered shrug in the brief silence that followed. "I just wanted to know how you're doing. And to let you know I'm going camping up in Vermont with a few of the guys in my dorm for a week after exams. Is that okay with you?"

Talia's insides turned to marshmallows. Kevin had always possessed the unique ability to mold her into a complete softy. "That's great. I'll miss you, but I'm glad you're getting away for some fun. How's campus life?"

"This semester's been tough. M.I.T. hasn't gained its reputation for being the top engineering school by coddling the students."

Mentally putting together a care package of cookies and other treats for him, she said, "You sound tired. Are you worried about your exams?"

"Nah, but I'll be glad for summer." He paused. "Listen Tal, I've got this professor friend. He teaches calculus. I told him about you, and showed him your picture—"

"Hold it right there, Kevin. If you're going to start matchmaking, more than your face will be in danger." She knew her brother felt responsible for her lack of dating partners during his high school years. Since she was financing his education now, too, he felt obliged to provide her with suitors beyond the realm of Barringer. "I'm doing fine," she added. "As a matter of fact, I'm getting ready to go to the country club in a few minutes."

Kevin gave a low whistle. "Who's the lucky guy?"

Talia rolled her eyes in self-disgust. She'd walked right into that hornet's nest. "Actually, it's part of the planning for Lung Awareness Month. I'm meeting a few people for dinner."

"Anybody I know?"

Studying her buffed nails, Talia grimaced. Kevin would be present for some LAM activities, so she'd better go ahead and break the news now. "Trace Barringer."

The silence was heavy, fraught with painful memories. Her heart twisted, and she rushed on. "It's not a real date, Kevin. For some reason I don't understand, Trace Barringer has been real pushy about this. I tried to put him off, but he's set on the idea of the mill being directly involved. If it were up to me, I'd tell him to take a flying leap, but the Barringer Corporation is one of our biggest contributors." She was breathless by the end of her explanation, and felt incredibly guilty and disloyal.

When Kevin didn't immediately respond, she said, "Listen, if it really bothers you, I'll resign from the committee."

His sigh was audible. "No. It just threw me for a minute. There probably isn't anybody who cares as much about LAM as you, Talia. Mom would be proud of you for what you're doing. Besides, Trace is the one Barringer who wasn't involved in my little mess with them. Val used to talk about him. She always said he . . ."

Talia strained to hear the uncompleted sentence. Kevin rarely spoke of Valerie Barringer, even though he'd been wildly infatuated with her years ago.

"Just keep your eyes open," Kevin warned her in a voice beyond his years. "We learned the hard way not to trust the Barringers." Then his tone lightened.

"I'll see you in a few weeks, big sister. And I'm bringing you a tall, dark, handsome guy with a brain as a coming-home present. The guys in Barringer are too stale for you. I love you."

"I love you," she whispered to the dial tone, and tried to work up some enthusiasm for Kevin's tall, dark "coming-home present." Unfortunately she was far more intrigued by a certain blond man with green eyes. She sighed heavily and snatched up her keys.

Alternately cursing and encouraging herself, Talia drove to Hidden Hills Country Club. When she stepped from her battered Datsun, she bit back a laugh at the parking attendant's expression of chagrin. She dropped the keys into the older man's hand and gave him a saucy smile. "Be careful with it, the front fender's a little loose."

When she looked up at the club's white columns and grand entrance, a tremor of unease swept through her. The differences between Trace Barringer's life-style and her own suddenly seemed acute. On her last date, she'd gone to a miniature golf course. Before that, it had been bowling. The most adventurous date she'd had in the last year involved a trip to Richmond to see a baseball game. And while she enjoyed baseball, she would have given her eyeteeth to see the opera.

Opera and ballet. Country clubs and elegant dinners. Those were Trace's life. Hers was ham and salami.

Still, Talia hadn't arrived at the age of twenty-six without a large dose of practicality. This country club would likely provide LAM with a generous donation. She battled down the notion that she was a fish out of water and marched up the steps.

Nodding briefly to the doorman, she muttered under her breath, "This one's for you, Mom."

She was crossing the red carpeted foyer, heading toward the desk to ask for directions to the lounge, when she felt a hand on her arm.

"Wait up, Italia," a familiar voice murmured behind her.

# *Three*

Talia whirled and stared up at Trace. Her heart sank with disappointment when she saw he still looked wonderful. She'd been hoping he'd grow a few warts during his time away. A man with his looks, intelligence, wealth, and insufferable self-confidence needed some flaw to bring him down to the rest of the human race. And she certainly didn't see a flaw. A charcoal silk blazer covered his impressive shoulders and chest, and well-tailored slacks fit his long legs perfectly. The light reflected off his tawny hair, and his green eyes glinted with humor.

What did he find so amusing, she wondered, then she remembered what he'd called her.

"Who told you that?" she asked as he led her down a hall.

"One of the supervisors at the mill. When I mentioned the plans for LAM, he casually passed on the information. Smiling wickedly, Trace opened the brass and glass door to the lounge. "I found it . . . intriguing."

"Did you happen to notice the guy's nose?"

Puzzled, Trace thought that over as they sat at a small round table. "Now that you mention it, Don's nose *is* a little crooked. Why do you ask?"

Talia smiled. "I went to school with Don. He's my best friend's husband. But he had this annoying habit of teasing me. I warned him to stop."

Trace watched the spark of indignation in her eyes and drank in the force of her personality. After another fruitless week spent trying to gain custody of his son, Talia was a breath of fresh air to him.

"Outside my family," she continued, "he's the last person to call me Italia to my face since seventh grade. I finally had to break his nose."

At the image of a feisty young Talia and a howling Don, Trace let out a deep laugh, feeling the tension leave his body.

"Can I get you something from the bar?" a waitress asked.

"Scotch, neat," Trace said, and turned to Talia.

"I'll take a Bloody Mary."

As they waited for their drinks, Trace noticed the way she looked around the room with carefully veiled curiosity. Dismay seemed to cloud her eyes, and she bit her lip.

"So what made your mother name you after Italy?" he asked in an effort to regain the earlier mood.

She turned to him, the bleak expression fading. "My grandmother died in Italy the week before I was born. Mom was devastated that she couldn't attend the funeral. And though my grandmother liked America, her first love was Italy. She was always telling my mother never to forget Italy."

Talia paused as the waitress set their drinks on the table. "When she first mentioned the notion of naming me after my grandmother's homeland, my father thought she was crazy with grief. But he went along with it, hoping she'd change her mind when it came time to fill out the birth certificate." Talia smiled and ran her finger around the rim of her glass. "She didn't. I'm just glad Grandmother wasn't from Turkey."

Trace grinned and watched the motion of her finger around the glass. "Imagine how many more noses would have been broken."

Her hands were small, he mused, but capable looking. She wore no fingernail polish, yet they still looked feminine. It was probably the way she fluttered them expressively when she talked. She trailed a finger through the beaded sweat of the glass, and his throat tightened. Amazing how sensual that gesture seemed.

"What are you staring at?" she asked.

He gulped down some Scotch. After debating how to answer, he opted for the truth. "The movement of your hand and fingers. I was imagining them in a different setting."

Her hand stilled abruptly. She wrapped it around the glass and took a sip. He could tell she was remembering his assessment of her breasts, and longed to pick up where they'd left off that day. He figured if he did that, though, they'd never make it to the dining room.

Keeping her expression blank, she said, "Tell me about who we're meeting tonight."

He complied with both requests, one spoken, the other unspoken. She wanted to keep the conversation platonic. He could handle that. "Two spinster sisters. The backbone of the country club. Martha and Prudence Fitzgerald."

"Oh."

Her tone had him studying her. What he saw surprised him. She wore a look of sheer dread. The realization dawned on him that she was nervous. He would never have believed it. She seemed so indomitable.

"Hey, they're not so bad," he said. "The only problem is that they both have memories like elephants. Prudence never fails to bring up some embarrassing incident from my childhood."

"Backbone of the country club," Talia repeated miserably. "Memories like elephants. In other words, if I spill my wine or drop my fork, they'll never forget it."

"Never ever," he said cheerfully. "But you don't need to worry. They'll be too busy telling you all about me. I don't suppose you've met them," he added hopefully. When she shook her head, he gave an exaggerated sigh. "I was kinda hoping you could take some of the heat."

His playful attitude teased a smile from her. He took that as encouragement to move to the dining room. After draining his Scotch, he stood and pulled her to her feet. "Come on. It's time to move into the trenches. By the way, you look great. Keep your legs out of my sight and I might have half a chance at saying something coherent."

An hour later, Talia was enjoying herself immensely. Though regal in manner, the two older women insisted upon being called by their first names. They also expressed interest in helping with LAM. And they dominated the conversation with stories about Trace.

Prudence shook her fluffy white head and clucked. "Yes, Trace had the worst case of diaper rash for the first six months of his life. It nearly gave his mother a fit."

Trace caught Talia's eye and put on an expression of great suffering. She bit back a laugh.

"Oh, I think his chicken pox was much worse," Martha said. "After all, he couldn't wear a stitch of clothing for three days."

The sisters bantered back and forth, each trying to outdo the other with their memories. After the tenth story, Talia had to admire Trace's indulgence of the sisters.

"Then again," Prudence said over coffee, "there was the incident with the poison ivy." She proceeded to expound on that particular ailment.

Talia smiled mischievously and leaned over to him. "Just think," she whispered, "if you were in outer space, you could scream without anyone hearing a sound."

Beneath the table, he snatched her hand and gave it a warning squeeze. Though he glared at her, she noticed he was fighting a smile.

It seemed peculiar to her that she could be so attuned to his feelings. She found it even more peculiar the way they'd taken turns studying each other throughout the evening. The glances said, "I like you" and "I want to know you better." In spite of her grudge against the Barringers, she couldn't resist Trace's sexy appeal.

She allowed him to lace his fingers with hers, enjoying the sensation of her hand being swallowed up by his. His was not the hand of a laborer. The skin was smooth, the nails well tended. But it was a strong hand. He rubbed his thumb against her wrist, and a tingle ran down her spine.

Glancing at him, she saw in his eyes a curiosity that matched her own. He moved his clever thumb again in a caress that caused a tightening in her stomach. He could see her surprise. She didn't know how she knew that, but she did. Clever hands, clever eyes. Her gaze fell to his mouth, and she couldn't help but wonder.

A question from Prudence drew their attention back to the sisters. "Yes," Trace answered, "both of my parents are"—Talia swept her own thumb across his palm. He stumbled and threw her a threatening glare. "—doing fine. Father is—"

She ignored the glare and experimentally stroked between his fingers. This time he glanced at her through hooded eyes, his gaze clearly saying, "You will pay." He laced his fingers firmly through hers. "Father plays golf every day. He's nearly fully recovered from his second heart attack."

Talia simply smiled. She'd learned something new about Trace that night. His hands were extraordinarily sensitive. And he didn't like losing control of a situation.

"Trace," a man said.

Trace looked up and saw his younger brother and wife approaching their table.

"Philip, Cynthia, what brings you here?" His hand automatically tightened around Talia's when she pulled against him. He didn't want to get into a wrestling match under the table, though, so he released it. As the sisters greeted Philip and his wife, he stole a glance at Talia. Her shoulders were stiff, her expression frozen. But her eyes flashed with such vivid emotion, he could tell it was an effort for her to control herself.

After charming the Fitzgeralds, Philip turned to Talia. Trace watched in amazement as Philip, the epitome of smoothness, faltered.

Coming to his brother's rescue, he stood. "Talia McKenzie, this is my brother Philip and his wife, Cynthia. Talia's in charge of Lung Awareness Month."

Philip nodded and pulled at his collar. Talia rose, her stance very erect, her speech clipped. "We've met."

Trace looked from Philip to Talia in bewilderment. An ugly feeling gnawed at him. "Oh, so you know each other."

Talia didn't spare him a glance, but held Philip under her steady gaze like prey. "We met six years ago."

Even Cynthia seemed to sense the tension. She slipped her elegantly manicured hand through the crook of Philip's arm. "Philip joined my father's law practice last year after we married." She smiled at her husband. "We're expecting big things from Philip. Don't be surprised when you see him entering the political area."

"Politics." Talia raised an eyebrow. "Somehow that doesn't surprise me."

Philip nodded again, but Trace noticed he didn't meet Talia's eyes. Philip cleared his throat. "How's Kevin?"

"He's a junior in engineering at M.I.T." The pride practically burst from her. "He earned a partial academic scholarship, and he makes the dean's list every semester."

"So, he's doing well?" Philip asked, sounding relieved.

A sea of emotions raced through Talia in the long silence that followed. She chose her words carefully. "Injustice does funny things to people. As a lawyer, I'm sure you know all about that. Some wounds never heal."

Trace was baffled. Following this conversation with all its underlying messages was like walking through a maze. At first he'd wondered if Talia and Philip had once been romantically involved. They were about the same age. Philip had never had any trouble attracting women, and Talia was the kind of woman who made a man gut-wrenchingly aware of his sexuality. Now, with all this talk about Kevin, he wasn't so sure."

"It was a pleasure meeting you both," Talia said to the Fitzgeralds, and grabbed her purse. "Please let us know what you decide about Lung Awareness Month. Thank you again."

She nodded in Trace's direction. "Good night."

He frowned. When she turned toward the door, he grabbed her arm.

"Wait. We're not finished."

She pulled away. "I've got to go. Thank you for dinner."

He suppressed a howl of frustration at her blank expression and cool, polite manner. In spite of her erect posture, her eyes looked as though she'd been through a war and lost. "I'll call you," he promised. He also vowed to get to the bottom of what was between Talia McKenzie and his brother.

After watching her leave, he turned to Philip. "I want to talk with you."

Philip shook his head. "There's no need, Trace. It's water under the bridge. Cynthia and I were just leaving."

Still, Trace noticed Philip wouldn't meet his eyes either. He would have pursued it, but neither the time nor the place was appropriate. When he wanted it, he knew he'd have all the information he needed. Letting it go for the moment, he escorted the Fitzgerald sisters to their taxi.

Moments later, he brushed the rain off his coat and started his Corvette's powerful engine. Driving toward the guest cottage on his parents' property, he brooded over the strained aura between Talia and his brother. The notion of the two of them together stirred a wholly unwelcome response in him. He wanted her for himself.

He'd taken one look at Talia McKenzie and something inside him clicked. It wasn't that she was the most beautiful woman he'd ever seen. His ex-wife was more conventionally beautiful. His ex-wife also wouldn't know an honest emotion if it bit her on the leg.

It was Talia's revealing face, her eloquent eyes. They were honest, and beautiful. That didn't mean she would never lie with words. But he knew intuitively that her face wouldn't lie. After the parade of cool, self-contained, self-assured women he'd known in the last several years, Talia was like—

His thoughts broke off abruptly when he heard a loud bang. The car jerked violently to the left.

"Damn!" Fighting for control, he slowed and pulled hard to get the car back into the right-hand lane. After he succeeded, he felt a sinking sensation when he correctly identified the problem.

He turned the car toward the curb. The rain poured down in sheets, lightning flashed in the distance, and his customized vintage Corvette had a flat tire.

It had taken Talia ten minutes in the ladies' room to come to grips with the emotions raging within her. She hadn't expected to see Philip Barringer that night. Whenever she'd visualized meeting him again, it had been with her hands wrapped around his throat. She commended herself for not murdering him on sight.

It was time to go home, she told herself. Time to forget about the Barringers. But when she pulled out of the parking lot, she remembered the events of six years ago with crystal clarity.

She'd warned Kevin to be careful with Philip Barringer, but Kevin had been young, naive, and in love. She still remembered the panic and fear she'd felt when she got the call from the sheriff, and when she saw her frightened brother in custody.

Then there'd been that ludicrous meeting with the court-appointed attorney. Finding little evidence to support Kevin's defense, the lawyer had suggested they throw themselves at the mercy of the court. Talia had been too naive to seek a second opinion.

Swallowing her pride, she had begged the Barringers to drop the criminal charges. Mr. Barringer had reluctantly yielded to her pleas, providing Kevin met certain conditions. Those conditions—which had included Kevin spending three months in a reform school so violent and poorly run, he had nearly been killed there—had irrevocably changed their lives. She would never recover from her guilt in consenting to the Barringers' legal maneuvering.

But the most tragic loss in the whole damn mess had been the death of Kevin's good faith and innocence. The young happy-go-lucky teenager disappeared, and no matter what she tried, nothing would bring him back.

Maybe if she'd been better informed, it would have ended differently. Maybe if she hadn't been so wrapped up in trying to get her own life on track, she could have prevented it. A thousand "maybe ifs" always ran through her mind when she remembered.

Talia shook her head and focused her attention on the rainy night. The dismal weather suited her mood. She narrowed her eyes when she spotted a man jacking up a car on the side of the road. A Corvette, she noted. It was fitting, she thought with uncharacteristic spite, that the owner of such an indulgent vehicle should have to change his flat tire in a downpour.

Still, her conscience wouldn't permit her to speed by. Although she wouldn't offer the stranger a ride, she could make a phone call for him when she got home.

She stopped and leaned over to roll down the passenger window. The man immediately turned around, her eyes widened in surprise when she saw it was Trace. She was tempted to roll up her window and drive away, but the sight of his drenched head and clothes roused an ounce of sympathy within her.

She sighed. "Okay, Mr. Barringer. Come on. I'll give you a ride home."

He moved closer to the car. "Talia," he said in amazement.

"Hurry up," she said. If she was obliged to do a good deed, she wanted it over with quickly.

Glancing back at his prized possession, he paused. "I don't want to leave it on the road. It won't take me but a few more minutes."

Talia rolled her eyes in disgust. Men and their cars. "For Pete's sake, you can pick it up before the rooster crows in the morning. Nothing will happen to your precious car before then. No one with any *intelligence* would be caught dead out on a night like this."

He hesitated a moment more, then nodded. "Okay, I'll move it farther onto the shoulder. Be back in a minute."

While he did that, Talia watched in her mirror for oncoming cars. Of course, there were none. Trace snatched his sport coat from the car, checked the locks, and swung into Talia's Datsun.

His shoulders were broader than she'd anticipated. In fact, his entire body was bigger. A sliver of unease fluttered in her stomach. His wet shirt clung faithfully to the impressive muscles of his chest, back, and arms. She swallowed and looked up at his face.

He flashed a smile, and his gaze fell to her damp dress. "Speaking of intelligence . . ."

Conceding his point with a nod, she drove forward. "I didn't feel like waiting for the valet." And she didn't like the way his gaze was lingering on the dress. "I don't know where you live. You'll have to point me in the right direction."

He sighed and relaxed in the seat. "I haven't had time to find a house yet. So I've been living in the guest cottage on my parents' property."

Great directions, she thought wryly. He'd made the correct assumption that everyone in Barringer knew where his parents lived, because everybody probably did.

"I'm surprised you know Philip," he said.

She stiffened and answered carefully. "He was a year behind me in high school." That was true, but she'd never spoken to Philip in school.

"Philip's always been popular with women. I think he usually spent more time juggling his dates than doing anything else. Must be his looks."

She mentally compared the two brothers and concluded that she preferred the sculpted angles of Trace's face to Philip's curved boyish features. Still, many women would find Philip's blond hair and calculated charm irresistible. "He's handsome, I guess," she said. "If you like that type."

"What type?"

"Uh, he's smooth."

"What do you mean?"

She sighed. "He's a little too smooth. I can't see

any rough edges with a guy like that. It makes me wonder what's really underneath. After all, no one's perfect."

Trace chuckled. "Well, I'll be damned." She stole a glance at him and saw he was shaking his head. "I thought he had everyone fooled."

Wanting to drop the subject, Talia was glad to see the entrance to the Barringer estate up ahead. She slowed to turn. "Which way to the guest cottage?" she asked when she reached a fork in the drive.

"To the right." Without missing a beat, he asked, "So what is Talia's type? Let me guess. A hardworking, honest guy who adores your Italian cooking and approves of your many earrings."

She felt her cheeks heat and reminded herself she'd be able to dump him at his doorstep very soon. Normally sensible, she allowed herself only a few eccentricities, one of which was her multi-pierced ears. She considered it a harmless expression of individuality. "Yes, to hardworking and honest. My earrings aren't usually an issue. And if a guy decides he wants me for my lasagna, he's gonna have problems. Kevin's the lasagna cooker in this family. I may make subs, but I have a passion for Chinese food."

She stopped in front of the cottage. "Here you are. Home again, home again, jiggity jig."

In the glow from the cottage's porch light, Trace could see the expectant expression on her face. She wanted him to slink away into the night. But he harbored an aversion to missed opportunities. "Come in for a drink. You can dry off."

"I'll dry off at home."

"Think of it as a small gesture of my appreciation." He got out of the car and walked around to her door, opening it with a flourish.

Taking in her distrustful expression, he smiled. "If

that doesn't work, think of it as a way to avoid future harassment from me."

"Can I have that in writing?"

"Of course," he said, and helped her out of the car.

"One drink," she insisted.

"One drink," he repeated.

Talia wondered why she felt as if she were being conned. Probably because she was.

Inside, Trace brought her a towel and a glass of wine. Then he excused himself to change his drenched clothes. Talia figured if she gulped the wine down fast enough, she could leave by the time he returned. But the soothing decor of the living room relaxed her, and she found she wasn't inclined to rush.

The room beckoned in a low-key way with a softly glowing brass lamp and muted green and blue color scheme. The casual decor surprised her. She would have expected formality. The striped pillow-tossed sofa looked entirely too inviting when she pictured Trace stretched out on it.

She moved to the bay window and stared into the rainy darkness. She'd only taken a few sips of wine when Trace reentered the room. Turning, she watched him approach her. The worn jeans fit him perfectly, molding powerful thighs and lean hips like a lover's hands. He'd left the top button of his cotton shirt undone, revealing a spray of brown hair. In the glow of the lamp, he was a study of masculine light and shadow. Talia's mouth went dry.

"Is the wine okay?" he asked, looking down at her.

"Fine."

Narrowing his eyes, he lifted a strand of her still-damp hair. "There's something very familiar about you. I would almost swear we've met before."

She wavered over revealing when they'd first met.

Would he laugh? She glanced down and shrugged. "Not likely."

"I guess not." He rested his hand on her shoulder. "So, what did you think of the Fitzgerald sisters?"

Her pulse tripped at his nonchalant touch, and she tried to answer in a normal tone. "They were nice. If you ever need a biography written on your childhood ailments, they're the experts."

He laughed. "Yeah, but I think they'll do a good job for LAM." He looked at the sofa. "Let's sit down."

She'd feel silly if she made a big deal out of it. After all, he wasn't inviting her to bed. The thought jolted her. "What would you say if I thought I might stay out of trouble if I remained standing?"

He trailed his palm down her arm and caught her hand in his. "I'd say someone has neglected your education." He led her to the sofa. "C'mon, Talia, give those pretty feet a rest."

She looked doubtfully at her sandal-clad feet as she sank into the cushions. "Pretty?"

He poured himself a glass of wine from the bottle on the coffee table. "Sure they are. They're slender and delicate with cute little toes."

Suddenly self-conscious, she curled her toes.

He sat down next to her. "And you know what that longer second toe means, don't you?"

She glanced at him skeptically. "I don't know. But this is beginning to sound like a palm reading."

"No, this is scientific. That longer second toe means you're very intelligent."

"I'll buy that," she said, and sipped her wine.

"Of course, it also means you're highly sensual and insatiable."

She choked and sputtered. When Trace thumped her on the back, she glared at him. "And which men's magazine did you get that from?"

He laughed. "A guy in my college fraternity had all these theories on how to distinguish the, uh, warm women from the icebergs. Something about your feet reminded me of that particular one."

At the very least, she should be offended by such an obvious ploy. She wanted *not* to like him. It would be so much easier. Instead, she was drawn in deeper by his charm, enticed by his sexy rumpled look. And when, pray tell, had a man complimented her feet? Fighting a smile, she asked, "How many times have you tried that line before?"

"Just once. It didn't work then, either."

She laughed at his dejected expression. "Should I offer condolences?"

"No," he said, suddenly serious. "I'm where I want to be."

# *Four*

---

Talia couldn't think of a response, so she took another gulp of wine.

Trace hooked a bare foot across the opposite knee. The V of his jeans stretched to accommodate the movement, and she'd have to be a saint or sightless to miss the impressive masculine swell. She was neither. She should have stayed at the window, she thought.

"I'm glad you came tonight," he said.

"Did I have a choice?"

"You always have a choice."

She shook her head. "Responsibilities can limit our options."

He brushed her hair behind her shoulder. "I understand responsibilities."

She didn't move away. His touch felt oddly comforting.

Stroking her hair, he spoke in a low, mesmerizing voice. "I wonder about you, Talia." His thumb grazed the three dainty earrings she wore.

It was an idle movement of his thumb against her

ear, she told herself. It shouldn't affect her so. Still, she found it difficult to breathe.

He continued caressing her ear. His breath fanned against her cheek. "I wonder if Talia took care of her mother when she was sick."

Growing warm, she swallowed. "Yes." A fist of wanting tightened in her belly.

Stroking his hand down her cheek to the little mole above her mouth, he stared at the mark as if fascinated. "I wonder if Talia took care of Kevin."

Her skin prickled pleasurably. She should get up, but his gaze held her, as if she were a deer stunned by headlights. Not trusting her voice, she simply nodded.

His finger traced the bow of her upper lip. "I know Talia takes care of her deli and LAM. But you know what I really wonder?"

Her mind was so clouded, he could have been speaking Chinese. His face was only inches from hers, and her heart pounded in a runaway rhythm. "What?" she whispered.

After placing her wineglass on the table, he leaned closer and their breaths mingled. "I wonder who takes care of Talia."

Automatically, she said, "I don't need—"

His lips landed gently on her open mouth.

It was like an extended, leisurely "Hello." Though her mind felt separated from her body, she remembered he'd once said something about not rushing. His firm mouth molded hers. He learned her pleasure by rubbing his lips against hers, tugging on her full lower lip, then sucking gently, tempting her to respond.

There was a second when she could have pulled away, but then he deepened the kiss. His tongue drew a circle of desire around her lips. He led her in a sensual duel, teasing her with light thrusts and parries of his tongue.

She forgot he was a Barringer. In the past few weeks, she'd fought fantasy after fantasy about him. The reality, she found, left those fantasies in the dust.

She gasped when he flicked his tongue over the mole he was so entranced with. He murmured his pleasure, and the sound of his deep voice rippled all the way down to her toes.

She'd never been lured with such care before. Bracing her hands on his shoulders, she joined in the seductive dance, opening her mouth to stroke his tongue with hers.

He groaned at the gliding motion, thrusting more deeply. He pushed her down on the sofa and followed her, drawing a breath of air. "Your perfume's enough to drive me crazy. What is it?"

Turning her head, she gulped. "It's French," she said. "I can't pronounce it."

He turned his mouth onto her neck, spreading hot kisses up to her ear. "I've got a thing about all these earrings." He ran his tongue over the tiny studs.

Talia was sure she was going to black out if he didn't stop. Her pulse was pounding in her head, in her chest, in her very core. If she had any sense at all, she'd roll off that sofa and run. But sense wasn't a factor. She wanted his mouth again.

Turning her head, she licked his lips, deliberately enticing him. With a low growl, he took control and sucked her tongue into his mouth. Talia gave and took, raking her fingers through his tousled hair.

He pressed his hard arousal against her and searched out her feminine curves. His heat only made her hotter until she thought she'd explode into flames. When had anyone affected her this way?

Her nipples peaked against his clever hands and she grew greedy. She arched into him. An intense satisfaction coursed through her as he groaned and ground himself against her eager hips. Her hands skimmed down his chest to where his heart thundered.

He pushed her dress up her legs and squeezed her thighs, then lifted his head. She whimpered at the loss and looked at him. His eyes burned hot. The thought struck her that she'd never seen green fire before.

"When I first saw you in this dress tonight," he said, his voice harsh, "I thought you looked beautiful. I didn't have any complaints when it was wet either. But right now, I want it off. I want everything off. Are you ready for what comes next Talia?"

She closed her eyes and waited for the room to stop spinning. She waited to cool off, but that probably wouldn't happen in this lifetime. Was she ready? She had known physical pleasure, but her limited experience had not prepared her for the storm of Trace's desire.

Choices. Either way she'd get punished. If she went ahead, her mind would kill her with regrets. If she didn't, her body would be aflame until she died.

She took a deep breath and allowed her mind to prevail. "This is difficult for me, but we've got to stop. I just can't do this."

A long silence swollen with suspended passion and emotion hung like a veil between them.

He clenched his jaw and pulled away. "It's too soon," he said. "If I'd been thinking with anything above my belt, I wouldn't have pushed."

When he moved off her, she had to bite her lip to keep from begging him to stay. Dammit, why couldn't he act nasty? It would be so much easier. "You didn't push," she said in a husky voice.

He helped her into a sitting position and brushed her hair from her face. "I'm not usually this way. But there's something about you, Talia, something about your smile and eyes." He tore his gaze from her red lips. "But we don't need to rush it. When can I see you again?"

She shook her head. "We can't."

"Can't?" he repeated, incredulous.

"That's right. It just wouldn't work, Trace. There are far too many—"

He grabbed her fidgeting hands. "You called me Trace." His voice held a note a triumph.

"It was a slip of the tongue."

He grinned. "Speaking of your tongue . . ."

"Trace," she warned, and pulled her hands from his.

"Talia," he mocked gently. "You can't convince me you don't feel anything when I touch you. We'd be crazy not to pursue this."

Exhaling a long breath. Talia rearranged her dress. He wasn't making this easy. She looked him directly in the eye. "It just won't work. There's too much bad blood between your family and mine."

His brow furrowed in confusion.

"Bad blood?"

"You really don't know, do you?"

"Know what?"

"I think you'd better talk to Philip."

His gaze was piercing. "What's the big secret? Why don't you tell me?"

She picked up her purse and stood. "You'd never believe me."

He stood too. "Try me."

That was the problem, she thought. She'd like to try him in all the ways a woman tries a man. Intellectually, emotionally, sexually. She was tempted to tell him what his brother had done to Kevin, but something stopped her. She sensed how disillusioned Trace would be when he learned of Philip's lies, and a deeply imbedded sense of fair play she'd never applied to the Barringers before kept her silent.

She felt an aching sense of loss for stopping their relationship before it started, but it wouldn't work. Tears leaked from her eyes. Mortified at such an emotional display, she swiped at them. How could her heart feel ripped in half when she hadn't given it away yet?

"Why don't I tell you?" she repeated shakily. "I guess because I don't want to be the one to hurt you. And if you have an ounce of integrity or family pride, if you love your brother half as much as I love mine, when you hear the truth, you're gonna hurt like hell."

With that, she fled to her car.

The following week passed in a blur of expended energy. On those rare moments when Talia's carefully erected shield of activity crumbled, her thoughts turned to Trace and she waged a furious internal battle against the memories of the way he'd touched her body and mind.

Touched, she berated herself, was an apt description. Touched, as in mentally ill.

It didn't matter that he made her heart race and her blood heat as no man had before. It didn't matter that he made her feel precious. It didn't matter that by word and deed he made her believe she was the most beautiful woman in the world.

It didn't matter, because it couldn't matter.

Trace had called her three times that week asking

to see her. Each time she'd forced her mouth to say "No," while a small voice inside her whispered, "Yes." At least she'd been honest when she'd turned down his invitation to dinner Saturday night. She'd told him she had other plans, and she did. A hot date with a guy with mischievous blue eyes, curly blond hair, and a fun personality.

At seven o'clock Saturday night, Talia found herself surrounded by the sound of bells, laser guns, and simulated jet engines. "Jason, isn't there something else you want to play tonight?"

"No," her four-foot-tall companion insisted. "I've been looking forward to playing the Reptile Renegades game all week. Aw, shoot! I keep getting phaser-dazed." Jason turned and fixed his pleading eyes on her. "May I please have another quarter?"

She fished another coin from her pocket and put it in his hands. Realizing she'd run out of quarters, she pulled out a few dollar bills too. "Here you go, sport. I'm going to get some more change. I'll be right back."

She turned and was heading for the change machine, when a pint-sized tornado whirled into her legs, yelling, "Reptile Renegades!"

The boy began to fall, and she instinctively reached for him, steadying his little body.

"Robby," a familiar male voice called over the roar of the arcade. "I told you to stop running."

Talia stared into the boy's green eyes. Her heart turned a somersault as she looked at the smaller version of Trace. She had no time to steel herself against the effect of Robby's father before he was standing in front of her.

"Robby," Trace began, then broke off when he recognized her. "Talia?"

Darn. Darn. Darn. Her gaze locked helplessly with

his for a timeless moment until Robby began to wiggle. Talia dropped her hands.

"Look, Dad, they've got Reptile Renegades. Can I play?"

Talia could practically feel Trace tear his gaze from her, and was glad she had a moment to get her bearings.

Trace gave Robby a quarter. "Wait a minute, Robby. It looks like somebody else is playing right now."

Watching Robby's face fall, Talia quickly said, "There's room. Four can play at the same time."

Robby immediately raced on to the game, Trace following him.

Talia went to the change machine, her mind racing a mile a minute. Every instinct she possessed screamed out warnings when Trace came around. Perhaps she could bribe Jason to leave, she thought without hope.

When she returned to the Reptile game, she was all set to haul Jason away.

"Fancy meeting you here," Trace said.

"Uh-huh," she said in a noncommittal voice, then tapped Jason on the shoulder. "Jason, you've been playing this game since we got here. Don't you want to try something else?" He gave her an uninterested glance, and she looked around the arcade. "How about Ghostbusters? Or the simulated jet flight? What about Skee-ball? I love Skee-ball," she finished a little desperately.

Jason regarded her solemnly. "Talia, if you don't like this game, I won't make you play. You can play Skee-ball and I'll stay right here."

He said it as if he were giving her permission, and she pursed her lips to keep from laughing. But when she heard the male chuckle behind her, she did laugh, over the whole situation. She'd spent the entire week trying not even to think about Trace, and here he was in the flesh, in a video arcade.

Jason and Robby seemed to be getting along wonderfully, she thought. It really wouldn't be nice to separate them. So it looked like she was stuck with three gorgeous males for the evening. Perhaps she could pretend that her history with the Barringers didn't exist. By his easy manner, she concluded that Trace hadn't learned about Kevin and Philip yet. And considering their two chaperones, it wasn't as if anything could happen between Trace and herself.

"Skee-ball or Ghostbusters?" he asked, holding out his hand.

Talia shoved the past behind her like dirt under the carpet. It was still there, but out of sight. She smiled and took his hand. "Skee-ball."

Several minutes later, Trace shook his head at all the coupons Talia had accumulated. "At this rate, the only way I'm going to be able to get Robby that stuffed animal he saw in the prize window is if I buy it."

"Buy it!" Talia exclaimed. "I can't believe you'd stoop so low. Every kid in here would be laughing up his sleeve if he saw you *buy* one of the prizes."

Trace grinned at her tone of horror. She finished up another game of Skee-ball, and he shook his head again, but this time at the view. The woman had the sweetest backside that encouraged all kinds of thoughts about things he'd rather be doing with her than playing Skee-ball.

Combing a hand through his hair, he promised himself the time would come. When she turned around and waved her coupons at him, he just barely stopped himself from kissing her.

"Okay, smarty-pants," he said, "just how do you suggest I get enough coupons?"

She shook her head sadly. "Trace, Trace. I can only conclude that you've led a horribly deprived life. If you knew anything about arcades, you'd know Ghostbusters is the only way to go if you need a lot of coupons."

She glanced at the boys, then asked, "How many do you need?"

"Three hundred."

She winced. "We'd better get started."

He hooked his arm through hers, eager for any closeness he could get. "So you'll help me?"

She looked surprised by the question. "Of course," she said, and squeezed his arm.

It was a little thing, but it stole another piece of his heart.

They checked on the boys a few times, but spent the next half hour busting ghosts with a light gun.

Seeing her like this made Trace even more curious about Talia and her life. "What would you do with these coupons if they were yours?"

"Would I have to pick something out of the window?" she asked.

"No. You could pick anything. Anything you like."

Talia cleared her throat, which had gone dry. His voice was like a caress, suggesting pleasure and tenderness. She wondered if he spoke like that on purpose, knowing what it did to her. She forced herself to concentrate on the game.

"If I had three hundred coupons," she said as she zapped a ghost, "I'd trade mine in for Chinese dinners delivered to my doorstep for a year."

"For three hundred coupons?" He raised his eyebrows skeptically.

"Sure, what about you?"

"I'll never tell."

"No?" She looked at him curiously. "Then let me guess."

"Go ahead. I'll give you a coupon if you can."

She cocked her head and considered the matter. "You look like a gourmet cuisine kind of guy. I'll bet you'd like French food delivered every night."

"No."

"Okay, I'll try the he-man approach. Steak and potatoes."

He just shook his head and smiled.

Lord, he thought, he loved being with her when she was like this. She reminded him of a curious little cat, slitting her eyes at him, trying to figure him out in a friendly way.

"Pizza?"

"You're getting close."

"Italian food," she said triumphantly.

He grabbed her hand. "You're getting very close."

Her breath caught in a short little gasp that nearly undid him. He watched her carefully, wondering if she'd give up the game out of shyness. She held his gaze, though.

"Something Italian?" she asked in a husky voice.

He nodded, looking deep into her eyes. "But I'm pretty sure it's something money or coupons can't buy."

"Me?" She said it as if she were actually considering the possibility.

He nodded again and raised his finger to her lips.

She shuddered visibly. Trace was glad he was touching her, so he could feel her response to him. She was much more susceptible to him than she'd let on.

"I'd like to get to know you, Talia McKenzie." The passion-rich emotion in her eyes made him want to lay her down and make love to her right there. "Inside and out."

A strip of coupons spat out from the slot. The bell signaling the end of the game saved Talia from doing something foolish, like leaning into the warmth of Trace's strong body and accepting his invitation.

She jerked her head to the side, looking away from his heated gaze. "The game's over," she said breathlessly. "We should have enough coupons for that little bear now."

"Timing is everything," Trace muttered, seeing that Robby and Jason were approaching them.

"Talia, " Jason said, "can we please play one more time?"

She shook her head and gave Trace the coupons without looking at him. "Don't you remember? We're going for ice cream." Relief rushed through her when she saw Jason's face brighten. Apparently ice cream was the only thing that could top the latest cartoon craze of the Reptiles. Perhaps she'd get out of the arcade while her mind was still intact.

"Ice cream!" Robby shouted. "Can we go too, Daddy?"

Oh no, she thought. She looked down at the little boy and searched for a gentle way to refuse. Robby, she could handle. It was his father she'd like to leave there.

Glancing up at Trace, she caught his expression of amusement. "I don't think . . ." Her voice trailed off when she looked at Robby again. She was such a sucker for children.

"Can we come too, Talia?" Trace asked, a wicked glint in his eyes.

Oh hell. "We won't be able to stay long," she warned, feeling outmaneuvered by all three of them.

"Great!" Jason said.

"Great," Trace echoed, taking her arm.

"What about the coupons?" she asked, trying to ignore her quickening pulse. "Don't you want to get the bear, Robby?"

"Gosh." He stared at the strips in Trace's hand, then looked at Talia's empty hand and frowned. "Well, what about Jason's coupons?"

Talia and Trace shared an expression of chagrin. Talia had gotten so caught up in being with Trace, she hadn't considered the inequity of the situation.

Robby's little eyebrows wrinkled in concentration, then his whole expression smoothed out. "Why don't we split them? What do you think, Jason?"

Jason liked that idea. Both boys snatched up their share of the coupons and ran to the prize counter. Trace halted the smaller boy and bent down to whisper something in Robby's ear that brought a smile to his little face. Talia's heart felt squeezed tight when Robby stretched his arm around Trace's neck and kissed him.

Trace straightened as Robby dashed off, looking after his son with an affectionate, proud light in his eyes.

"Pretty impressive," Talia said.

He turned to her and nodded. "That's what I told him."

And another stone fell from the fortress around Talia's heart.

Everything was going fine at Walton's Ice Cream Parlor. The boys had conned a double dip out of the adults without too much trouble. While Talia splurged on a hot fudge sundae, Trace opted for a root beer float.

"Jason will be getting a new brother or sister any day now," Talia informed Trace.

Trace glanced at Jason. "Is that so? I bet you can't wait."

"Yeah, I'm really hoping for a brother. Getting a sister would be awful," Jason said, and rubbed his chocolate-smudged nose.

"Hey," Talia said in mock offense. "I'm a sister and you don't think I'm that bad."

Jason grinned. "Nah, but you don't act dumb like most girls. It's probably 'cause you've got a real neat brother like Kevin."

Talia laughed. "I'm sure Kevin would agree with you."

"When's he coming home? He promised to take me to the lake this summer."

"He'll be home in a few weeks," Talia assured him. "He's taking exams, then going camping with his friends."

"In New England?" Trace asked, remembering Kevin attended M.I.T.

"Vermont."

"Kevin's great," Jason said, "but he doesn't smile very much."

Talia's stomach clenched. "He used to smile a lot," she murmured.

The group fell into silence. Unaware of the tension, Robby continued mauling his melting lime sherbet. Jason concentrated on scooping up his last few bites.

Trace thought of the phone calls he'd made to Philip, phone calls his brother hadn't returned. Wrestling with his impatience at being left in the dark, he twirled his straw through the float and looked at Talia. "Did Kevin change when your mother died?" he asked gently.

She drew a deep breath, the kind of breath a person takes when she feels tired or burdened. "Some. It was really the next year, though, when . . ." She broke off, and her sad expression tore at him.

With lips and cheeks covered in green, Robby suddenly said, "Daddy's got a brother. He wants to be President and Daddy's going to help him."

Talia sucked in a quick breath and pushed away her bowl of ice cream. Her stomach would revolt if she forced down one more bite. She'd pretended she bore no animosity against the Barringers, but it had taken only a couple of innocent comments to bring reality crashing down.

She was frustrated with the tug-of-war she felt when she was around Trace. On the one hand, she couldn't dismiss what the Barringers had done to Kevin. On the other hand, she was having a hard time dismissing Trace's strong appeal.

"Time to go, Jason." She turned to Robby. "It was nice meeting you. Your daddy's very lucky to have you for a son."

Robby grinned. "I know."

She forced a laugh, tousling his hair. "I just bet you do. I guess I'll see you at the next LAM meeting, Trace."

She wouldn't meet his eyes, Trace noticed. She stood, looking as if she were ready to run. He knew he couldn't stop her, couldn't fight what stood between them until he found out what it was. But he could give her something to think about in the meantime.

He stood too. "You're forgetting something."

After wiping Jason's chin, she finally looked at him. "What?" she asked, her voice edgy.

He clasped her hand and pressed a coupon into

her palm. Her hand trembled the way he predicted her body would when he made love to her.

Her eyebrows drew together in puzzlement. "What's this for?"

He smiled. To make sure she understood him, he spoke with deliberate temptation and challenge. "Whatever you want."

Her cheeks flushed as she tried to shove the coupon back at him.

"You're blushing," he murmured.

"I never blush," she shot back, her embarrassment turning to anger. "I'm not fair enough to blush."

"Whatever you say," he said.

Talia was tempted to pick up her bowl of ice cream and dump it on his handsome head, just to wipe that insufferable grin off his face.

She let the anger guide her. It was the only clear emotion in her bloodstream at the moment. Like a cornered animal, she struck out, going for Trace's jugular.

"The only thing I want from any Barringer," she said with lethal precision, "is money for my charity. They have nothing else to offer me."

She immediately felt like pond scum.

Unable to meet Trace's gaze, she clasped Jason's hand and pulled him firmly to the door. Deliberately hurting Trace made her stomach churn with guilt and regret. But she had to make it clear there was no future for them.

She was certain she'd dampened his ardor, hurt his ego, until she heard his taunting voice.

"Chicken."

# Five

Not one word. That was exactly what she heard from Trace Barringer after Saturday night's ice cream. Sometimes Talia wondered if instead of hearing him softly call her a chicken, she'd just dreamed it.

It was a sad day when a Barringer called a McKenzie chicken and got away with it.

Sadder still, her conscience chided, when it was the truth.

She was beginning to feel like a very inept opponent in this battle for her . . . for her what? Virtue? She laughed out loud at the thought.

She'd technically lost her virtue five years earlier during her one puny attempt at a serious relationship. Between helping Kevin recover from his ordeal and taking over the sub shop, there'd been little time for romance, and the young man had grown impatient with her responsibilities.

It must not have been too serious, Talia had concluded, because when he'd called it quits, she'd felt more relief than regret.

She just wished she felt no regret over Trace

Barringer. But she had never been good at lying to herself. The blatant invitation Trace extended with his sexy voice and eyes was almost too tempting.

So she spent the next several days trying to brainwash herself. She figured if it worked for governments and religious cults, it might work for her. Her best hope lay in the fact that Lung Awareness Month would be over in five weeks, and her ties to Trace Barringer severed. She carried out her daily activities while chanting "Just five more weeks," and when that didn't work, she listed Trace's faults. He was arrogant. He had a bad memory. He was too rich, too well educated, and too handsome. He had a smart mouth. Thoughts of his mouth, however, brought such sensual images to mind, she had to abandon that part of her plan.

By the time the next LAM meeting rolled around the following Wednesday night, Talia glumly concluded she wasn't a good candidate for brainwashing. She would just have to set the tone for a more businesslike relationship between them.

The issue of Kevin would always stand between them, she told herself. When it came to their social worlds, she and Trace moved in different galaxies. While he spent his day directing a multimillion-dollar corporation, she spent hers serving ham and turkey sandwiches.

Arriving home late from the shop on Wednesday put a pinch in her schedule. In an effort to fight the humidity, she threw on a pair of red shorts and a white T-shirt, then pulled her hair back into a ponytail.

After crossing herself in thanks for the fuses not blowing, she pulled a pan of chocolate chip cookies from the oven. She couldn't resist the enticing aroma for more than a minute and popped one into her mouth.

She howled at the burning sensation. *That's what you get for rushing,* she scolded herself.

Someone knocked on the door.

She headed for the living room with half the cookie in her mouth and the other half in her hand. Pausing she panted to cool the cookie, then gulped it down.

She opened the screen door with her free hand, licking her lips. When she opened her mouth to say hello, she saw that it was Trace and no sound would come. Her heart slammed into her ribs.

He stood on her brick doorstep wearing his lethal smile, a white shirt that gave peeks of his throat and muscular forearms, and a pair of jeans that knew his body as intimately as she'd like to.

"Hi," he said as his gaze roamed over her.

"Hi," she managed over the lump in her throat. Her mind scrambled for its automatic defense mechanism.

"I need to—" she started.

"I wanted to—" he said at the same time.

They both laughed self-consciously.

"Listen," Trace said, "if you're not going to eat that, I haven't had dinner yet." He looked meaningfully at her right hand.

She glanced at the hand as if it were unattached to her. "Oh, the cookie. You can have it." She gave it to him. "I have plenty more in the kitchen."

Walking toward the small kitchen, she rolled her eyes at her awkwardness. "The rest of them should be cool by now," she added over her shoulder. "I got a little eager and fried my taste buds right before you came."

Abruptly remembering her need to put their relationship on a more businesslike footing, she turned around to face him. "Trace, I—"

There was a knock at the door. She frowned in frustration and started back to the front of the house.

"Hey, wait a minute." Trace shot out a hand to stop her. His eyes narrowed as he studied her.

Shifting uncomfortably, she joked, "What's wrong? Have I got a smudge of chocolate or something?"

Moving closer, he rubbed his thumb across her cheek. "As a matter of fact, you did."

Her cheek suddenly felt as if it had caught fire. She watched him lick the bit of chocolate from his thumb and felt the rest of her body heat.

Hearing another knock, she forced herself to turn toward the door, wondering at the strange light in his eyes.

"Guardian angel!" he called after her in a deep, astonished voice.

The words fell against her back like stones, stopping her in her tracks. She felt a flush of sheer pleasure and she didn't even try to respond. She couldn't explain why it was so important to her that he remembered, but a giddy relief sang through her.

And a thousand chants of "five more weeks" bit the dust.

She managed to walk on to the door and open it. "Hi, Opal. Come on in." She marveled at her calm voice when her insides felt like a bowling alley on tournament night.

Trace scarfed up another five cookies, helped himself to a glass of milk, and chatted with the other committee members. He sat in the lumpy blue chair again and kept his gaze on Talia the entire meeting. Every once in a while she threw him a bewildered little smile that made him feel incredibly predatory. Especially considering his latest scheme. He couldn't take full responsibility for all of it. The Fitzgerald sisters had given him a perfect opportunity. He'd just developed it to suit his purposes.

After experiencing Talia's temper, he wondered if her shy smiles would turn to furious glares when she heard his plans. He predicted she wouldn't give him the full brunt of her temper until the rest of the committee left. By then, though, he'd have her committed to sharing the entire weekend with him.

Guardian angel. He shook his head, staring at her while Darryl droned on about some plans at a local bar. The ponytail had tipped him off. He'd had the unsettling feeling of déjà vu around her almost from the beginning. The fact that she was the one who'd run into those thugs so long ago only made her more appealing to him.

"So, it will be a kind of western dance night minus cigarette smoking." In one sentence, Talia summarized what Darryl had taken twenty minutes to say. "So, the first week of Lung Awareness Month, we'll have information booths set up at the local grocery stores and the town square where people can pick up pamphlets and candy for the children. Health officials are taping spots for television and radio announcements, and the state president of the National Lung Association will make an appearance that first week.

"The second week"—she glanced at Trace for approval—"the mill is sponsoring a skating party, with all the proceeds going to LAM."

When Trace nodded, she continued. "The third week is the western dance and smoke-out. And," she added tentatively, "you asked us to reserve the fourth week for something at the country club, Trace."

Leaning back, Trace wished for a stiff drink. He had a feeling he was going to need it. "The Fitzgerald sisters contacted me yesterday. They've decided on a charity auction. And they're all excited about a donation they might receive for it. It's quite valuable. But there's a catch."

Talia was thrilled with the prospect of more donations. "That's wonderful."

The other committee members nodded in agreement. Only Lou seemed to hear Trace's last comment. "You mentioned a catch," he said.

This was where the bottom fell out, Trace thought. "This valuable donation will be given by the Fitzgeralds' youngest sister, Camilia. Years ago, she married a senator and moved to Washington, D.C. Her husband died a few years ago, but she has stayed active in Washington society with her charitable contributions. Prudence and Martha say she's a bit eccentric," he added with an ironic smile.

That was like the pot calling the kettle black, Talia thought, grinning too.

"Anyway," he went on, "she wants us to come for a weekend visit that will include a press conference and a party. Apparently Camilia loves publicity."

"Exactly what is she donating?" Lou asked.

"An antique Aubusson carpet, previously owned by an English king."

"We've got to go to D.C. for a rug?" Lou said in disgust.

"Not all of us," Trace said, and turned his gaze to Talia. "Just Talia and I."

The committee seemed to breathe a collective sigh of relief. Talia, however, felt a bolt of sheer terror at the thought of a press conference and a stuffy Washington party. "Me! Why me?"

The question left her lips before she realized she'd already received her answer. Trace wore that lazy predatory expression she'd glimpsed a few times that evening. First suspicion, then indignation flared through her. That scheming, manipulative . . .

Ready to lash out, she glared at him, then caught her breath. His expression might be predatory, but his eyes held such hunger, she had to turn away.

"Apparently," he said, "Camilia wants the head of the committee to receive the carpet personally. And she also wants a Barringer around, since Barringer is her hometown."

Talia's heart raced at the prospect of an entire weekend with Trace Barringer at her disposal. Or would she be at his disposal? Either way, the mere thought sent shivers of fear and pleasure down her spine. How could she possibly keep her distance from him in those circumstances? Especially, her conscience chided, when she didn't want distance.

Alarmed at the thought, she pushed it aside. "This is very unusual, Trace. And I do have a business to run."

Opal piped up. "I'd be glad to help you out, and you've got your part-timer to fill in for you."

"Yes, but—"

"Before we get all in a dither," Lou interrupted, "just exactly how much is this *rug* worth?"

Trace almost smiled at Lou's blunt question, but he shared the businessman's attitude toward the bottom line. And he predicted the bottom line would end all of Talia's protests.

"One hundred and fifty thousand dollars," he said.

They all gaped at him.

"A hundred and fifty big ones," Lou muttered. "Hell, I'd be willing to walk to D.C. for that."

Darryl cleared his throat. "Well, you simply must go. We'll take care of your sub shop. Do you have the proper clothing?"

Still reeling from the amount of the gift, she blinked at Darryl, then realized he'd directed the question to her. "I'm sure I'll manage something," she murmured, though she had no idea what.

"Oh, Lord," she whispered, realizing she'd just committed herself to going. She really had no choice, she told herself. Swallowing down the lump in her throat, she asked, "When do we leave?"

Trace saw her struggle with confusion, anger, embarrassment. Right now she looked ready to face the guillotine. "Camilia has summoned us to meet her early Friday afternoon." He improvised his plans just in case she needed to do a little shopping. "If you don't mind, I thought you could go to a museum or do some shopping while I take care of some business downtown before we go see her. We'll leave early Friday morning and return on Sunday. The party's Saturday night."

"This Friday?" she asked weakly.

He nodded, feeling a smidgen of sympathy for her. She'd caused him too much frustration for him to feel too sorry for her, though.

"Oh, this is so exciting," Opal said as she stood. "I want you to remember everything about the party so you can tell us all about it."

Darryl and Lou stood as well and started toward the door. "Don't worry about your shop," Lou said. "We'll take care of it."

Talia nodded absently. The shop was the least of her worries. She bade her guests good-bye and, after closing the door behind them, turned to face Trace.

"Go ahead and get it over with," he said.

"What?" she asked blankly. She was still wondering what she was going to wear and when Trace had figured out how they'd first met.

"The screaming and the yelling. I could tell you were about to go off like a firecracker when you realized what I'd done."

"Oh." She nodded in understanding, remembering her earlier vexation. Gazing at him, she thought he looked unusually restless. "You mean now is when I'm supposed to tell you what a miserable, dirty, manipulative, low-down snake you are."

He winced. "Something like that."

"And how you took advantage of me to suit your purposes. That you were sneaky and underhanded by telling me about the Fitzgerald donation in front of the other committee members. Because you knew," she continued doggedly even though he clenched his jaw, "I would sooner walk through—"

"I think you've made your point. I'll see you Friday morning." He walked stiffly around her.

"Trace," she said, barely suppressing a smile, "there is just one more thing."

He stopped, but kept his broad back to her. "What?"

"What took you so long to remember how we met?"

The sound of crickets filled the momentary silence as Trace slowly turned. He'd braced himself for another strike from her tongue. Instead, she stood in front of him with her hands on her hips and full of feminine pique that he hadn't remembered her. Seeing that small display of vulnerability tugged at his protective nature. He started toward her.

"I remembered the important things," he said, wanting to please her.

She arched her eyebrows skeptically.

"I remembered your courage, your sense of humor." He grinned and brushed back a loose strand of her hair. "I remembered your ponytail.

"But I also remembered you as a child." He ran his thumb down her cheek to her lips. "And now you're a woman with all kinds of charms and secrets that have me half out of my head."

She let out a soft, trembly sigh that tried his self-control. He gazed into her eyes and felt he was staring at his destiny. "We need this trip." When she started to protest, he shook his head and pressed his thumb against her lips. "We need it so we can be just Talia and Trace. Not Barringer and McKenzie."

He slid his hand to the nape of her neck and pulled her to him. "Just you and me, Talia, for three days. Deal?"

A sea of emotions rose and fell like the tide within her, but her desire for Trace remained the strongest. Perhaps it was no longer desire, but need. When she accepted that, an odd peace enveloped her. "Deal," she answered, unable to think beyond this special moment.

He nodded, then kissed her.


They made their escape at dawn and forgot about responsibility and bad memories. They shed their last names and became Trace and Talia. It was wonderful.

She learned that he preferred any kind of home-cooked meal over restaurant food because he ate out so often. He learned that she preferred restaurant food because she prepared food all day long. They shared a smile over that and privately thought of ways to compromise.

They both avoided any discussion of Philip. Talia was relieved. Did he know yet? she wondered once, then brushed the depressing subject from her mind. In spite of the luxurious Cadillac they rode in, she could almost forget the differences between them, because Trace kept the conversation light and easy.

She finally asked him why he'd worn tinted glasses that morning she'd met him in his office. He explained that he'd just gotten back from the eye doctor, and drops had made his eyes sensitive to light. He normally wore contact lenses.

"You've got great eyes," she said honestly.

He flicked those great eyes over her and said, "You've got great everything."

When they arrived in Washington, Trace pulled into a downtown parking garage and cut the engine. "I've been wanting to do this for at least a hundred miles," he said. He leaned across to kiss her, then nuzzled the sensitive spot just below her ear.

Talia didn't even think to push him away. Closing her eyes, she clutched his strong shoulders and savored the sensation of his firm mouth against her skin.

"You know," he murmured, "you never did tell me what kind of perfume you wear."

She sucked in a quick breath and drew away. "I told you it's French. I can't pronounce it."

He grinned. "Then why are you blushing?"

"We've discussed this before," she said, grabbing her purse. "I don't blush. Shall I meet you in an hour?"

He watched her fumble with the door. If she weren't so charmingly unsettled, he'd consider pushing the issue. "An hour would be fine."

Later that afternoon, they drove to Camilia Wentworth's estate not too far outside the city. Everything seemed to go well. Accustomed to hostessing, the grande dame put Talia at ease. Trace made both of the women laugh. And Talia didn't embarrass herself by spilling tea.

But how had she been persuaded to go horseback riding? she wondered later, as she stood in borrowed riding clothes near a freshly painted stable. The tea cakes she had just eaten sat heavily in her stomach. "Trace," she whispered, "this is not a good idea. I've never ridden before."

"Never?"

She nervously eyed the black stallion the stable hand brought out to him. "Never. The only horse I've ridden was wooden. It did not eat."

Trace nodded and turned to the stable hand. "We need a gentle mount for the lady."

"Sure, I've got just the one," the man replied.

"It's really not that difficult," Trace told her with easy confidence. "These horses are probably so well trained they need little direction. Just keep your knees and toes in and your heels down. If you need to stop, simply pull the reins in." He squeezed her stiff shoulder, but she did not feel reassured. "You'll be fine. And Camilia might fork over another donation if we take a little ride with her."

"This is not a good idea." She rubbed her damp palms together, realizing this was a prime example of the incompatibility of their life experiences. Trace had probably owned pedigreed horses, while she'd never even ridden one. What if she fell off? What if she embarrassed Trace? He should have brought someone else this weekend, someone more accustomed to tea parties, cocktail parties, and horseback riding.

"It's a great idea." Trace patted his mount. "Think

about how you rode into those hoods who were trying to beat me up."

"I was riding a bike," she reminded him.

Impatient to be off, the stallion stomped and whinnied. The scent of leather and horseflesh filled her nostrils. She backed away, briefly considering tapping her boots together and saying, "There's no place like home."

The stallion stomped again, and Talia broke into a sweat. Visions of getting kicked or bucked raced through her mind. "I'm going to die," she whispered.

"Talia," Trace said sternly, "I won't let anything happen to you. Now look at your mount. Doesn't he look gentle?"

Talia took a deep breath and looked at the brown horse being led to her. He didn't look too wicked. "What's his name?" she asked.

The stable hand smiled reassuringly. "Satan."

She would never walk normally again.

Even after soaking in the Jacuzzi in her hotel room until her skin wrinkled, Talia was sure she would never walk normally again. The "little ride" Trace had suggested had extended to two hours of derriere-breaking torture. On the positive side, Camilia had donated a Ming vase to LAM.

At least her room, with its thick plush carpet, cherry furniture, and soft lights, provided a soothing ambience to her aching body and frayed nerves. She lay, carefully positioned, on her stomach on the large bed, almost asleep.

There was a knock at the connecting door to Trace's room. "Room service," he said.

"I didn't order anything," she called.

"It's Chinese," he answered in a tempting voice.

The man knew her weaknesses. Sighing, she dragged herself from the bed, wrapped a robe around her poor body, and opened the connecting door. Trace held a bottle of wine, two glasses, and three white take-out cartons.

"Your color's a little better," he said, looking her over. "You were white as a sheet when the groom told you your horse's name was Satan."

"How was I supposed to know it was a misnomer?" she grumbled.

He smiled. "I shouldn't tease you. You did great. I had no idea Camilia would keep us so long. Did the Jacuzzi help any?"

"Some."

She watched him pull a small table to the foot of the bed and pour the wine. He turned the radio on to a soothing station, then shut off all the lights except one. Talia's heart hammered against her rib cage.

He walked over to her and reached for her hand. "Come on and eat. You look like you're about to fall over."

"Trace, I can't," she said, trying to pull her hand from his.

"Can't?" He frowned and noted her uneasy stance. Glancing around the room, he saw that while he had attempted to create a relaxing atmosphere, she'd misread it and assumed he was going for seduction. And if she didn't look so miserable, that was exactly what he would be doing.

He contained the chuckle bubbling within his chest and pulled her to him. "You've got the wrong idea. As much as I like the idea, I don't think you're in any shape for a tumble in bed. I'm just trying to get you to sit down to eat."

Pushing against him, she made a little sound of frustration. "I can't."

He began to feel worried. "Can't. You can't what?"

She looked at him with such forlorn eyes, his heart melted. "I can't do anything, even if I want to."

If he read her correctly, "anything" meant making love and she wanted to. His body immediately responded.

"I don't even think I can sit," she added.

He winced when he realized the extent of her problem. "Damn. I forgot how sore you get the first few times you go riding. I should have stopped Camilia after an hour."

"No. It's okay, and we did get the Ming vase," she said in an unconvincing tone.

"Ah, Talia." He hugged her. "Let's see if lying on your tummy will work. Maybe some wine, food, and a back rub."

So she followed Trace's orders and stuffed herself with sweet-and-sour chicken and cashew shrimp. After sipping two glasses of wine, she was past drowsy, but not quite drunk.

For the next fifteen minutes Trace rubbed his magical hands over her shoulders, back, and bottom. The effect was both soothing and stimulating. In other words, frustrating, and instead of relaxed, Talia felt cranky and vulnerable.

"Why are you doing this, Trace?"

"You said you were sore." He continued the tender massage, willing himself to keep his mind on the massage, even though he wanted to remove her silky robe and nightgown and do something else entirely.

She sighed into the pillow. "No, I mean why have you been giving me the rush? There must be scads of women who'd be more suitable for you. Ouch!"

His hands had dug into her skin, and he immediately gentled them. "Suitable," he repeated.

Talia couldn't see his face and was deceived by his

calm tone. "As in wealthier, better educated, et cet— Ouch!" She turned around to look at him.

Trace removed his hands from her completely, since he was considering wringing her neck. He caught her wary expression and took a breath to gain some patience.

"What does wealth and education have to do with a woman I might want? For that matter, who's to decide what is suitable for me?"

Talia closed her eyes against the fury in his gaze. "Nobody should decide what's suitable for you," she admitted. "I—I guess I just don't understand the attraction. I mean . . ." Her voice shook alarmingly. "I have a correspondence-school certificate. You have a law degree. I'm not wealthy. You are." She shrugged and opened her eyes to look at him.

Trace truly would have wrung her neck if she hadn't looked so vulnerable. "I could tell you those things don't matter to me, and that would be true."

She still looked so doubtful, he had to smile. He brushed her hair back from her forehead. "I could tell you I've had a thousand fantasies about that little mole above your mouth, about feeling your skin against mine, about your legs wrapped around me. And that would be true, too." He watched her cheeks heat and her eyes darken, and cursed a horse named Satan.

Leaning next to her, he placed a soft kiss against her lips. Her eyelids fluttered. "Your honesty and courage impress the hell out of me."

He stroked a finger along her jaw and gazed into her eyes. "But I think the real reason is that I haven't been lonely since we met."

Talia closed her eyes, but the tears welled up and over anyway. Heedless of her soreness, she reached for him, pulling him into her arms. "Oh, Trace," she murmured. "No one has ever—" Unable to finish, she took a deep breath.

He snuggled her warm body into his arms. "What? No one has ever taken care of Talia?" She nodded. "Then I'd say it's about time, isn't it?"

She parted her lips, seeking his. It was a generous kiss, full of poignant emotion that led to passion. His mouth explored, giving more than she'd ever dared to dream.

And she gave to him, more than he'd ever dared to hope. When they broke apart, their breathing was shaky, and she said only one word. "Stay."

# *Six*

Sometime in the middle of the night, a tingling in her arm woke Talia. She could have shifted her arm and gone back to sleep. Instead, she realized her head rested on Trace's bare chest, which was rising and falling in an easy rhythm.

She wanted to identify every sensation of being held by Trace Barringer and save them up for some cold, lonely night when her arms were empty again.

Both of his arms were wrapped around her protectively, almost possessively, one behind her neck and the other over her hip. His grip was relaxed, but she sensed that if she moved, he would tighten his hands.

Her own hand curled against his chest. She felt the steady thud of his heartbeat. His chest hair tickled her cheek. She nuzzled against him, inhaling the compelling combination of his cologne and masculine scent.

With a will of its own, her hand slid over his chest, exploring the muscles, the whorls of brown hair, the male nipples.

His hand snaked from her hip to catch her wandering one. He brought it to his lips, kissed it, then placed it back over his chest.

"Not sleepy anymore?" he asked in a rumbly voice.

His heart was beating faster, she noticed. She shifted back to look at his face and stretched.

"My arm fell asleep. It woke me up." She fluttered her fingers over his whisker-rough jaw to his lips, smiling at the sight of his sleep-tousled hair. She would remember that too.

He rubbed her shoulder. "How are you feeling?"

"Better," she said, surprising herself. Earlier she'd wondered if she would ever feel better.

His hand stilled and he looked at her intently. "How much better?"

She knew what he was asking. She also knew he was giving her a choice, even though he was already aroused. With their lower bodies pressed together, she felt the full evidence of that fact against her thigh.

She could call it quits and later say she'd done the practical thing. But if she was going to remember Trace Barringer on cold, lonely nights, she wanted more than bits and snatches. She wanted it all.

With that in mind, she eased up and kissed him. "Much, much better," she murmured.

He didn't ask again, but placed her hand against his thundering heart so she could feel his response.

They used no words, but spoke eloquently with their eyes. He turned her gently until she was beneath him, then began a devastating assault on her mouth.

After teasing the seam of her lips with his tongue, he took jabbing little thrusts into her willing mouth. The room spun and she clasped her fingers behind his head, joining in the dance, fusing their mouths to savor his darker flavor.

Her breathing was ragged when he finally pulled away to unbutton her silky nightshirt. All her anxieties about her body rushed to the forefront until she remembered the time in her store. The time when he'd told her in exquisite detail what he'd like to do to her.

As if he were recalling that also, he gave her a heart-stopping grin and flicked his thumb across the tip of one breast. She felt the jolt down to the pit of her stomach.

"I dreamed you'd be like this," Trace murmured, enjoying the play of his hands against her receptive nipples. "Soft. And hot." He molded his large hands to her flesh, and stroked and tempted until her skin was flushed and she arched into him.

He groaned at her instinctive sexual movements. If it weren't for that scrap of lace covering her femininity, he'd be slaking himself in her velvet sheath that instant. The lure of her tested his self-control. But he wanted this to be right for her.

Lowering his head to her small, high breasts, he kissed and tasted her, then sucked a rosy bud into his mouth. She whimpered and moved restlessly beneath him.

"Trace," she whispered, and clutched his shoulders as a hollow feeling settled low in her belly.

He brought his mouth back to hers, this time with less finesse and more need. Moving his arousal against her yielding form, he gave her a tantalizing hint of what was to come.

She grew more adventurous and slid her hands down his chest, past his flat belly to the edge of his briefs. He sucked in a deep breath when her hand lingered at the elastic barrier. Then, sensing his need, she pushed beneath and took him into her hand. She squeezed, then stroked with loving fingers.

"Oh, Lord, you're incredible," he rasped.

She'd never been so bold before and had only imagined acting with such reckless abandon. With Trace's response encouraging her, she pushed the briefs down his legs until he could kick them off. With his gaze consuming her, she urged him onto his back and took a journey down his body with her mouth and tongue. She tasted his neck, then kissed his nipples, nipped his belly, and nuzzled his thighs.

Trace was half out of his mind with her. She'd ignored the part of him that swelled and ached for her, teasing him unbearably with the sweep of her hair as she made her way down to his feet.

She kissed behind his ankle, his knee and thighs again and hovered over the essence of him. He gritted his teeth at the picture she made, tousled hair, dark hazy eyes, swollen lips. The beaded tips of her breasts pressed into his straining thighs.

She looked at him for a moment, and it struck him that she was just as aroused as he.

Talia stared into green eyes naked with desire and shivered. Then she lowered her head.

And Trace went straight over the edge. She attended to him with kisses and caresses, running the tip of her tongue up the length of his throbbing shaft and robbing him of his very breath.

His chest heaving with exertion, he dragged her up and fastened her mouth to his, then he removed the last barrier between them. When her hands began to wander again, he firmly circled her wrists.

"Just one moment," he said huskily. "Or it will all be over so fast your head will spin."

"My head is spinning," she said.

He cursed, though it sounded more like a prayer, then he rolled her onto her back and returned measure for measure. Enticing her relentlessly with a tongue that ignited and hands that stoked the flame, he made her his. He kissed every inch of her, until their bodies grew damp with perspiration, and she was frantic with the building tension. She wanted him so much.

"Trace," she whispered.

"Soon," he promised, and caressed the pearl of her femininity until she was moist and swollen with need.

"Trace," she cried as he drove her closer to insanity, "I need you."

He was gone for only seconds as he pulled the protection from his slacks pocket. Joining their hands on either side of her head, he stared into her eyes and slid his thighs between hers.

His face held such intense desire that for a moment she panicked. She lay before him, a bundle of feminine need and vulnerability. It was just Trace and Talia now. She felt completely at his mercy, until she saw the evidence of forced control—his clenched jaw and uneven breathing.

She lifted her hips in invitation.

He accepted, sinking his body into hers, inch by excruciating inch, until there was nothing between them. His fullness in her tightness. She grew light-headed.

"Tonight you're mine," he whispered.

She closed her eyes at his words, but he wouldn't allow it.

"Look at me," he said tenderly.

When he withdrew, she tightened her legs around him instinctively.

"Tonight I'm yours." He thrust deeply and muffled

a groan. She shuddered as the coil within her tightened.

He withdrew again. "Say it."

"Yes," she whispered brokenly, knowing her soul
had been taken along with her body.

Trace's control was spent. He plunged deep into
her, leading her into a depth of passion, both terrifying and glorious, chasing sensation after sensation. Then he thrust one last time, and they both
cried out as the tempest snatched them into ecstasy.

Trace lay heavily on Talia, his face wedged into the
curve of her shoulder, breathing as if he'd raced a
freight train. He expelled another shuddering breath
and squeezed her.

"Good Lord," he muttered.

Talia was having difficulty catching her own
breath, let alone talking.

Raising his head, he looked at her. He touched her
cheek as if she were fine porcelain, and concern
edged into his eyes. "You okay?"

She nodded.

A slow grin spread across his face. "You look kinda
phaser-dazed."

She smiled faintly, recalling the fate of the Reptile
Renegades whenever an enemy defeated them.
Phaser-dazed was exactly how she felt.

Moving to her side, he gathered her in his arms
and stroked her hair. "I'd really like to know what's
going on inside your head right now."

She turned so she could look at his face. "I don't
know what to say."

"How do you feel?" he asked, searching her eyes
for answers.

"Devastated."

"You're not alone."

She wanted to believe him, wanted to believe he was as deeply affected as she. But she couldn't prevent her doubts.

Some of her uncertainty must have shown through. "You don't believe me, do you?" he asked.

She sighed. "Well, Trace, I'm not exactly widely experienced. I'm sure you've had more . . . involvements."

"Nothing in my whole life comes close to what we just did."

"But your wife—"

"Nothing."

She shivered at his resolute tone.

"And I'm glad you're not widely experienced," he said, chucking her chin with his forefinger. "I don't think I'd like sharing you."

"Is that so?" The corners of her lips turned upward. He sounded so much the territorial male.

"It is," he said, his expression still fierce. The thought struck her that maybe even the great Trace Barringer needed reassurance sometimes too.

"Well." She drew out the word and rolled over onto his chest. "You know, you've got droves of competition. There's—" She stopped, unable to come up with even one other man's name in her present flesh-against-flesh position. She shrugged helplessly. "Well, there're just too many to name."

"So many men littering your sidewalk, you probably have a hard time getting to your car in the morning." He clucked sympathetically and settled her along his long, hard length. "Must be a rough life."

Biting her lip to keep from laughing, she saw by the gleam in his eyes he was getting into the spirit of the conversation.

"Oh, it is," she assured him. "But you are"—she paused, assessing him carefully—"passably handsome."

"Passably?" He lifted one of his dark eyebrows.

"More than passably."

He waited in silence.

"Oh, all right. You're incredibly handsome."

He grinned.

"And as a lover—"

He shifted beneath her until his hardness pressed against the apex of her thighs. She drew in a weak breath.

"—you're," she tried to continue, but he moved again. She could feel her nipples beading in the hair on his chest. His arousal pressed against, but did not enter, her femininity, and she started to turn to liquid.

"Yes?" he prompted.

It would only take a slight movement, she thought, and he would be inside her. Her mind was as hazy as early morning fog.

"I forgot what I was saying."

He trailed his hand down to her bottom and lightly stroked. "You were saying something about what kind of lover I am."

She looked at him blankly, and he took pity on her. "Maybe this will help," he said, and slipped inside her.

He watched her close her eyes in an expression of rapture and almost came right then. Only his earlier release gave him the control to hold back. He lifted his hands to her soft breasts and turgid nipples, gently squeezing.

She arched and took him in more deeply.

Groaning, he brought her mouth to his for a wet, hungry kiss.

She lifted, then sank down the length of his swollen shaft again. They both trembled. He reached down into her warm, damp curls, and flicked the sensitive spot, once, twice.

She lifted. He plunged. They both exploded.

A minute later she opened her eyes and whispered, "Unequaled."

Although she tried to hide it, Trace detected the stiffness in Talia's gait the next morning. She was sore, he realized, and he'd bet it wasn't all from the horseback ride. So, after separate showers, he hustled them out for sight-seeing.

It was a golden day he'd never forget, filled with laughter, fun, and easy conversation. He was surprised at the pleasure he took in the little things, like holding her hand as they toured the Smithsonian. It made him feel young again, like a teenager on a first date, so eager to please.

After lunch, as they strolled past shops, he noticed Talia's attention straying to the windows. "Let's go in," he said, and gently pushed her into the closest store.

It was a jewelry shop, and for the first time he realized that she wore no jewelry except her earrings. It bothered him enough to want to alter the situation. His first instinct was a ring, a ruby for her passionate nature, or perhaps a diamond. A diamond that could later accommodate a matching band.

*My God, what are you thinking?* He took a deep breath and stared at her as she fiddled with some costume bracelets.

She must have sensed his gaze, because she looked up at him and smiled. His heart lodged in his throat.

"You're bored, aren't you?" she said. "I appreciate

the effort, Trace, but I don't know any men who enjoy shopping." She hooked her arm through his. "We can go now."

He blinked. The feeling was too new and too strong. He'd have to deal with it later, when he had time to sort it all out.

"I'm not bored," he assured her, and thought for a moment. "What are you wearing tonight for the party and press conference?"

"A two-piece dress. It's magenta colored. Why?"

He was already pushing her over to another counter. "I'd like to get something for you to wear with it."

"Oh no, you can't," she said in a horrified tone.

"May I help you with something, sir?" a salesman asked.

"The diamond necklace over there." Trace pointed.

"No!"

Both men looked at her as if she were crazy.

"You don't like diamonds?" Trace asked.

"No. I mean, yes. Oh!" She sighed in frustration. The situation had gotten entirely out of hand.

"Diamonds are nice, but it really isn't necessary for you to buy anything for me."

"But what if I want to?"

"I still don't think—"

"If she doesn't prefer diamonds, perhaps she'd like something like this." The salesman pulled out a delicate gold chain with five graduated filigree hearts.

"Oh," she murmured, this time in pleasure. It was beautiful and she'd never owned anything like it. She reached out to touch it just for a moment, then drew back her hand. "I really can't."

"Talia." Trace took her aside and looked at her in

a way that made her knees melt. "I want you to have something that will remind you of this weekend."

"You say that like you think I could actually forget it."

"Indulge me. It's just a necklace, not the Hope Diamond. Or did you see something you liked better?"

"No," she said quickly. "It's beautiful. But—"

"We'll take it," Trace said to the salesman.


That evening Talia got her first taste of a high-class Washington cocktail party. Camilia's ballroom had mirrors on every wall, reflecting the sumptuous elegance of original artwork, fine crystal, quiet-voiced servers, and a fountain of champagne. Talia smiled to herself. The only original artwork her family had ever possessed had been crayon drawings on the refrigerator.

At first she'd been overwhelmed by the famous people she recognized, by the glitter of exquisite jewels, by the fabulous designer gowns. Fearful of making some horrible social gaffe, she'd stiffly gripped a glass of champagne and smiled and nodded a lot. Trace had loosened her up with sotto voce anecdotes about the people she met.

During one of the few quieter moments, she relaxed enough to notice that he seemed restless. She touched his arm to get his attention. "Anything wrong?"

"Hmm? Not really," he said, and slipped his arm around her waist.

"Then why did I have to ask you that question three times?"

He looked surprised, then repentant. "I'm sorry. I

talked with Robby this afternoon and he mentioned that Madelyn is in New York again, so her mother is taking care of him. I was sure Madelyn would be ready to give me custody by now."

Talia could feel his impatience and frustration as if it were her own. "Why don't you visit him tomorrow before we leave?"

His gaze held a mixture of tenderness and fire. "You know, you're not just the most beautiful woman in this room tonight." He bent down to kiss her. "You're the nicest."

A lump rose in her throat, preventing speech. She leaned against him and watched desire flare in his eyes.

"But at this moment," he growled in her ear, "I'm not thinking about anything but getting you out of that dress." His hand slid down her hip, drawing her closer.

"You don't like it?" she asked, knowing her shiver belied her light tone.

Grinning, he eased them back a few paces into a dimly lit corner. "I like the dress. I like the way the top—" He stared at her breasts and stopped. "What kind of top is it?"

Over a very dry throat, she said, "It's called a bustier."

"Bustier?" he repeated, his grin turning wicked. "That's appropriate, considering it doesn't cover all of your—"

"Trace," she warned in a shaky voice.

"Right. Well, I like your . . . bustier." His hands spanned her waist, then slid down to her hips. "And I love the way it fits here." His voice grew husky. "But it's a little long."

She blinked. The dress ended three inches above her knee.

"The slit in the back helps," he continued, and sneaked a kiss behind her ear.

Between his caressing hands and devouring gaze, Talia was having difficulty breathing. Still, she managed to catch his hands when they strayed too far. "The way you talk about this dress makes me wonder just what kind of clothing you prefer to see on a woman," she muttered.

"Let's just put it this way," he said, pulling her against him. "Seeing you in this dress makes me think of all the different ways I could get you out of it." He put his mouth against hers and whispered, "And all the different things we could do once it's off."

The rest of the evening passed in a magical daze for Talia. She felt like Cinderella without a curfew. Even the press conference came off without any glitches. Trace handled the journalists without a qualm, and Talia only had to answer a few simple questions. Camilia was the real star, milking the presentation of the valuable carpet and Ming vase for all she could. Talia was counting the minutes until they could leave, when everything came crashing down.

"Trace," a familiar voice said from just behind her shoulder. A chill ran up her spine, and she stiffened. It couldn't be.

Trace turned and smiled at his brother. "Philip, I didn't know you were coming."

Philip looked at Talia, then glanced away. "I couldn't miss it. It's a great opportunity to make contacts." He nodded toward a photographer and put his arm around Trace's shoulder. "The publicity won't hurt either."

Philip smiled as a lightbulb flashed. "You want to get together for drinks after this is over? I keep trying to talk you into being my campaign manager for my run for the state senate. I shouldn't have to nag my own brother."

Trace shook his head. "If you'd take no for an answer, you wouldn't have to nag. Besides, you know you can count on Barringer Corporation for a generous contribution."

Talia left, quickly and without a word. If she didn't lose her dinner over the way Philip was using LAM to further his political career, then she'd lose it over learning that Trace planned to underwrite him. Sick at heart and not quite sure where she was going, she wandered through the crowd, murmuring, "Excuse me, excuse me, please."

She ended up at the front door. When the butler asked if she needed a limo, she almost burst into tears. What was she doing? She couldn't leave without thanking Camilia again and saying good-bye.

She closed her eyes for a moment and pinched the bridge of her nose.

"Miss, is something wrong? May I help you?" the butler asked in a kind voice.

She sighed, opened her eyes, and gave the elderly man a tremulous smile. "If you could arrange for a taxi, I'd appreciate it."

"Of course. How soon will you require it?"

"Umm, five or ten minutes. Is that possible?"

He smiled. "Anything is possible at Miss Camelia's."

Somehow, she made it back through the crowded ballroom to Camelia and thanked her again.

"Why, darling, it's been my pleasure," Camilia said. She gave Talia a little hug. "I'll have to think of something for next year. You know, I believe you paid dearly for that Ming vase. You haven't danced a single dance with your divine Mr. Barringer."

Talia's stomach turned.

"I shouldn't have let you ride so long," Camelia fretted charmingly.

"Oh, no," Talia said. "I enjoyed it."

"You don't lie well, my dear." The older woman studied Talia for a moment. "But you're a strong woman. It's been a pleasure meeting you."

Even in the midst of her misery, Talia was flattered. "It was my pleasure too. Thank you for everything." Impulsively, she kissed the older woman on the cheek, then dashed away.

Trace looked around the room as Philip continued to pressure him about the political campaign. Frowning, he muttered to himself, "Where the hell has she gone?"

When Philip sighed heavily, he turned his attention back to his younger brother. "What's the problem?"

"Nothing," Philip said, "if you don't count the fact that I've used my most persuasive abilities trying to win you over to run my campaign for the last ten minutes. It doesn't look good for my future if I can't sway my only brother."

Impatience flashed through Trace, but he reined it in. He was accustomed to Philip's self-centered attitude. "Look, I'll support you financially. I'll give you advice." He grinned. "For what it's worth, I'll even give you an endorsement. But Philip, you need to understand that I've got some big things going on in my life right now. I'm about to get custody of Robby and I just might lose my mind over a certain lady. So don't ask me again. I said no and I mean no." He put his hands on his hips in vexation. "Where the hell is she?"

"You mean Talia McKenzie?" Philip asked.

"Yes. Who else?"

Philip shrugged.

The silence between them seemed loud in contrast to the conversations surrounding them. Trace turned and looked at his brother closely.

Philip glanced away. "You might want to watch out. The McKenzies seem . . . ambitious."

"What do you mean?"

Philip shifted from one foot to the other. "You know what I mean. Some people will do anything to get ahead. They'll use relationships, affection, even sex—"

"That's enough," Trace said tersely. A dark anger built within him. Philip's insinuations put a tawdry light on Trace's relationship with Talia. It took all of his control not to lash out. "Speculations made from ignorance always cause problems, little brother. In other words, don't discuss things you know nothing about."

Philip stiffened and met Trace's gaze. "I know plenty about the McKenzies. This isn't the first time they've tried to worm their way into our family."

He turned to leave, but Trace grabbed his shoulder. "You owe me an explanation after that last comment."

Angry color flared in Philip's face. "I don't have to tell you a damn thing. As far as Talia McKenzie is concerned, you'd better keep your head on your shoulders and your money in the bank."

A hot surge of nearly uncontrollable fury hit Trace like a fist. "If you weren't my brother, I'd knock your teeth down your throat." He took a deep breath, fighting for calm. "Now get out of my face before I do something I regret." Dropping his hand from Philip's shoulder, he watched his supremely cool brother shakily back away.

Trace cursed as his usually agile mind raced fruitlessly. Why was Philip so hostile to Talia?

It made him wonder anew if Philip and Talia had once been involved. The insulting way Philip had spoken of her infuriated him. He'd been an inch away from tearing a strip off Philip. The only thing that stopped him was the possibility that Philip might reveal what was at the bottom of this mess right in front of all the reporters.

Thinking about that only raised more questions that couldn't be answered, and Trace felt a swift, searing need to see Talia. He shook off his disturbing thoughts and looked around the room once more. She'd been gone entirely too long.

He checked the champagne fountain, the corners of the room. He even asked a woman to check the powder room. Finally, he asked Camilia.

She frowned. "Well, she said good-bye to me a while ago. I assumed you'd made arrangements to depart separately."

Doing anything separately from Talia had been the furthest thing from his mind. He thought they'd planned to be together for the rest of the evening, straight through till morning if he had anything to do with it.

He smiled stiffly. "Thank you again, Camilia. I hope you can make it to the auction."

"Oh, I will try," she assured him as a senator's wife cornered her.

Spying an elderly butler, Trace paused at the door. "You haven't seen a dark-haired woman in a magenta dress, have you? She's about this tall." He held his hand up. "She's got brown eyes and a little mole above her mouth."

"Wearing a necklace with little hearts?" the butler asked.

Trace's heart raced. "Yes."

"She left about thirty minutes ago. I called a cab for her."

# Seven

The knocking on her door was getting louder.

"You might as well open up, Talia. I'm not going anywhere," Trace yelled through the door.

"It's been a long day," she called back. She looked down at the tissue she'd completely mauled and cursed softly. "I'm tired, Trace. I really don't feel like talking."

"That's too bad," he said without one drop of sympathy. "Open up."

She stared impotently at the door.

"Talia."

"Oh, all right!" She tied her robe tighter, mentally girding herself for the battle she knew was coming. She'd only been in her room long enough to discard her clothes and take a quick shower. When she'd spied the heart necklace still on her neck, she'd practically ripped it off. It was a glaring reminder of how foolish she'd been to forget the barriers between Trace and herself.

She walked stiffly across the plush carpet, flung the door open, then stepped back and crossed her arms over her chest. Her first tactical error was looking at him. Exasperation-mussed hair topped a grim, yet achingly tender face. His eyes were so full of hurt that guilt began to seep into her.

"Is there any particular reason you left without me tonight?" he asked in a quiet, controlled voice.

She shrugged and turned away, moving back into the room. "I got tired. It looked like you were enjoying your time with Philip, so I didn't want to interrupt."

She felt the vibration of one heavy footstep before he jerked her around and clasped her shoulders. She flinched at the expression on his face. The tenderness had vanished, replaced by fury.

"It's over," he bit out.

Her heart dropped to her knees.

"All this evading the issue," he continued, "running whenever Philip shows up, is over. I want to know what's going on and I want to know now."

Shaking her head, she tried to back away.

He stopped her by tightening his hands. "Now."

"No, Trace, I can't. I told you why."

"I don't care why you think you can't." He ruthlessly stripped away her defense. "I deserve to know why you were all over me at that cocktail party and now you can't bear to talk with me, let alone touch me."

Her cheeks flooded with heat. "You know why. It's Philip. Seeing him brought it all back, and I just couldn't deal with it."

He loosened his hands slightly and began to move his fingers in a caressing motion. The gentleness she'd grown accustomed to crept back into his eyes, his voice. "Brought all of what back?" he asked in the voice that never failed to turn her to putty.

It almost worked. She opened her mouth, ready to tell him anything he wanted to know, then a shred of reason permeated. He should hear this from Philip. She shook her head and looked away. "I can't—"

He stepped back and cursed.

"Why not?" he asked in a harsh voice that chilled her blood. "Are you sure you're not making a big deal out of nothing?"

That gave her a start. Her gaze whipped up to meet his.

"What's the big secret?" he went on. "Did you and Philip have an affair? I can't believe you'd be the type to play the scorned woman for this long."

Talia was speechless for a moment.

"Affair? Scorned woman?" she said in a high-pitched voice. She gave a choking laugh and felt her fury rise. "Oh, I wish that was all it was. Big deal out of nothing," she repeated incredulously, and shook her head.

With righteous anger oozing from every part of her, she narrowed her eyes and practically spat the condemning words from her mouth. "My brother spent three months in a hellhole, got stabbed, and came out a shell of his former self. All due to your precious brother Philip."

Trace looked like she'd slapped him. "There must be some mistake," he finally said.

Talia was on a roll now. "Yeah, there was a big mistake and Philip engineered it real well."

Trace's brows pulled together in confusion. "Not Philip. You can't be sure."

"I couldn't be more sure."

He shook his head. "No. I can't believe—"

"That's exactly why I haven't told you," she said with bitter triumph, and turned away. "You've got your story. Now get out and leave me alone."

She sank down on the bed before her knees betrayed her. A lump rose in her throat when she realized she'd destroyed any chance for a future with Trace. But there'd really never been a chance, she reminded herself. She hugged herself tightly as if to ward off the cold. Staring down at the bedspread, she noticed for the first time that the flowers were orchids. She concentrated on the green leaves and pink petals, willing the time to pass until the door closed behind Trace.

But Trace didn't leave. Instead, he sat beside her and took her cold hand. "Please," he said, "tell me the whole story."

She opened her mouth to refuse, then looked at his face. It was bare of anger and judgment, stark with vulnerability and need. She sensed that such vulnerability was rare for him. And he'd become too important to her to push him aside cavalierly. She couldn't take away his pain or her own, but he desperately wanted the truth. And she desperately wanted to give him what he wanted, even if it drove them apart.

Unable to look at him, she stared down at her clasped hands and told him how Philip had engineered Kevin's arrest.

"They closed the reform school a few years ago," she finished later, "due to mismanagement and health code violations."

Trace stared at Talia and fought against overwhelming, painful bewilderment. He didn't know what to think, but he didn't want to believe Philip was capable of such deceit. The horror and senselessness of the deed appalled him. "Are you sure you didn't misunderstand? Could you have misinterpreted something he said or did?"

She shook her head. "The whole thing went too smoothly not to be planned. You're a lawyer, Trace. You know how difficult it is to prove something like this. Especially against someone whose name is Barringer," she added bitterly.

Her lost expression made his gut clench. "I'm a Barringer."

She looked up with tears in her eyes. "Yes, but you're everything he isn't."

He took a deep breath. Standing, he shoved his hands into his pockets. "I don't know what to say. It seems unreal. I don't think you'd lie," he assured her quickly. "But Philip— I can't understand why he'd do something like this. He was always protective of Valerie, but this is out of character."

Seeing his confusion hurt her further. "Trace, I know this is hard for you. But surely you can see why I've insisted that things won't work between us."

His head whipped around, his eyes piercing her to her core. "As a matter of fact, I don't."

She lifted her hands. "Trace, your family is everything to you. And Kevin is everything to me. This can only destroy us."

"No!" The rush of sheer panic surprised him. The problem with Philip was disturbing, but the mere suggestion of Talia slipping away from him was untenable. A cold chill swept through him. "You're wrong," he said, coming back to her side. "My family may mean a lot to me, but they're not everything. This can only destroy us if we let it."

"Philip is your brother."

"He's not me." He wanted to shake her, but cupped her chin instead. "This happened years ago. We have to deal with the present." He gazed into her misery-filled eyes. "Or are you determined to live in the past?"

She looked away. "It's not that easy, Trace. Even if your brother hadn't tried to destroy my brother, we'd still have all these differences between us. Your life is completely different from mine. Our social circles will never mix."

"We mixed pretty well last night. You came apart in my arms and I came apart in yours." He saw the doubt and confusion in her eyes and wanted to kiss it away, but he sensed it wouldn't work. He'd have to find the right words. "And it isn't just sex," he continued, correctly guessing what was going on in her mind. "I've waited too long for this, maybe all my life."

Her eyes widened in alarm, and he bit off an oath. She still didn't want to admit how important they'd become to each other. "Tell me, Talia, have you ever felt like this before?"

He saw the fire dance in her gaze before she closed her eyes and shook her head. "It doesn't matter," she said. "It can't matter. There are too many—"

"Too many other people's needs?" he interrupted, barely reining in his impatience. "What about what you need? What about what I need?" He shook her gently. "When will the time be right? When will everything be perfect so you can let go and take a risk?" He paused because he knew he had her attention. Her eyes, full of worry, were fastened on him.

"Never," he said, answering his rhetorical question. "And never's not good enough for me." He took her hands again and comforted himself with the fact that they trembled. Then he played his last card, knowing Talia rarely backed away from a challenge. "Is never good enough for you?"

"Oh, Trace." She let out a shaky sigh and looked at the ceiling. He watched her blink against the shiny tears forming in her eyes. "I don't know."

He still wasn't satisfied. He wanted more. But when the phone interrupted the silence, he told himself "I don't know" was better than a definite no.

Talia answered it, then handed the phone to him. As he listened to a hospital receptionist, he wondered what else could go wrong that day. He closed his eyes, clearing his mind and battling fatigue.

"It's the hospital," he told Talia as he hung up the phone. "Something's happened to Robby's grandmother."

Over the next hours, Talia was amazed at how time alternately crawled and sped by. They were at the hospital in a matter of minutes. It was by unspoken request that she'd come along. And she found she wouldn't have it any other way. She was thrilled to have Trace depend on her.

While Trace spent hours on the phone trying to locate Madelyn in New York, Talia reassured Robby about his grandmother. She had fallen down the steps and broken her leg in two places. She went immediately into surgery at the hospital, where they inserted some pins. Recovery, the doctor predicted, would be slow.

By late Sunday afternoon all three were headed back to Barringer in Trace's Cadillac. Talia sat in the back seat with Robby, because he'd looked so forlorn by himself. His little body was stiff with tension, but finally, after four books and three songs, he snuggled against her. His eyelids began to droop. "Talia, you smell so good," he said.

She smiled. "Well, thank you, Robby."

"You smell just like bubble gum. Do you have any?"

She blinked. Catching Trace's eye in the rearview mirror, she laughed. "If he keeps up these compliments, he's destined for permanent bachelorhood."

"Oh, I don't know. His technique may need a little

work, but his heart's in the right place." Trace lowered his voice. "I can't fault his taste."

She looked back at Robby and started to answer his request, but he'd already gone to sleep. Brushing the blond hair off his forehead, she marveled over what a beautiful child he was. He already had the same dark eyebrows and eyelashes that Trace had. Frowning, she noticed he also had dark circles under his eyes. It had been a tough night for everybody.

"Out for the count?" Trace asked quietly.

After securing a pillow beneath Robby's drooping head, she leaned toward the front seat. "He's gone," she murmured. She startled herself by almost reaching out to stroke Trace's face in an offer of comfort.

"Give me your hand," he said, as if he'd read her mind.

He kissed her hand, then leaned his whiskered cheek against it. They rode that way for a long time in quiet contentment. Talia didn't want to examine that feeling too closely. She might destroy the peace and serenity of the moment. Still she couldn't think of anywhere she'd rather be than in the back seat of a car with a four-year-old boy, while her arm fell asleep because Trace Barringer insisted on holding her hand.

The Cadillac ate up the remaining miles to Barringer. Robby was still asleep when Trace stopped in front of Talia's house. She couldn't resist giving the sleeping child one last kiss before she got out.

"I'll get your suitcase," Trace said in a low voice.

She nodded, feeling strangely reluctant to leave the car. But she did leave as quietly as she could.

Trace followed her up the walk. The night air was thick with humidity, and only the sounds of a neighbor's dog and chirping crickets broke the silence.

She'd left the porch light on. It illuminated the big crack in the concrete walk that she hadn't had a chance to fix yet. She needed to mow the yard too. Maybe she could squeeze it in tomorrow evening. She hadn't noticed how dingy the paint looked either. But it was clean, her prideful side asserted. And it wasn't cracked or peeling.

Suddenly she realized why she was noticing all the little faults in her home. Trace Barringer. She'd spent the weekend pretending to be Cinderella, eating caviar, drinking champagne, and getting drunk on Trace's attention.

But the ball was over.

The Cadillac coach would be gone in just a few moments, and she would be left with her Datsun pumpkin.

But what about the necklace? her softer side argued. What about the way he held you in his arms? That had to mean something.

It meant they'd had a great weekend, she answered herself. Trace and Robby were going back to the Barringer mansion where they belonged while she remained there where she belonged.

Funny how that short walk from the car could make a world of difference.

She sighed, then turned to face Trace when she reached the door. After all they'd been through in the last twenty-four hours, she felt like weeping at the prospect of not being with him and Robby any longer. If she could just avoid looking into Trace's eyes, maybe she could avoid making a fool of herself.

Pasting a smile on her face, she fixed her gaze on his chin. "Well, I can honestly say I've never had a weekend quite like this," she said lightly, and tried not to think about their endless lovemaking on Friday night. "I think the committee members will be pleased about the carpet and the vase." Of course, mentioning the vase made her think of horseback riding, which made her think of Friday night again. Her composure started to slip.

"Talia—"

"Thanks for everything, Trace," she rushed on. "I would have felt like a fish out of water if you hadn't been there. Although Camilia was very nice." She twisted her fingers together, still refusing to look at his eyes. But his chin was too damn close to his mouth.

"Talia—"

"Listen, Robby will probably wake up any minute." She practically jerked her suitcase from him. "He might get scared and—" He put his hands on her shoulders. She might have pulled it off, but she blew it by looking up into his mesmerizing eyes.

"Talia, I can honestly say I've never had a weekend like this either," he murmured in a velvety tone.

Goose bumps rose on her skin. She clutched the suitcase handle tightly, as if hanging on for dear life.

"I want to see you again soon, but Robby . . ." His voice trailed off and his face wore regret.

A lump rose in her throat, and she forced another smile. "I understand, Trace."

His eyes narrowed. "Do you really?"

"Of course." If she couldn't erase her doubts, the least she could do was conceal them. Trace had enough on his mind. "You'll be terribly busy. Robby needs you right now. He needs you to make his life as stable as possible."

Trace nodded. "You're right about that. I feel like I've got to make up for this whole last year."

He seemed so burdened, and a wave of compassion swept over her. "You two will be fine. He's so happy to be with you."

"Think so?"

"Sure," she said, and deliberately lightened the discussion. "Especially if you get him that puppy he wants."

Trace grinned and her heart wrenched. He pulled her closer and kissed her once, twice, then released her and looked down at her with his searing gaze. "I'll be in touch."

"Of course," she said huskily, and hoped she sounded much more confident than she felt.

He cupped her chin in one hand, however, and studied her face. "I will call," he said as if the words should be etched in stone.

Her throat was tight, so she simply nodded and blinked away the shaming moisture in her eyes.

He frowned. "Is something wrong with your eyes?"

"Oh, they feel a little gritty from lack of sleep. That's all." She turned away and magically produced the key from her pocketbook. Some supernatural force enabled her to insert it into the lock and turn it.

Just before she cleared the threshold, Trace wrapped his arm around her waist and kissed her on the top of her head. "See you later."

She nodded, holding her breath until his arm was gone. The tears were falling before she'd closed the door behind her.


Over the next week, whenever Trace had a free moment—and that was rare—he remembered his last conversation with Talia. Something about it nagged him. She'd said all the right things. She'd kissed him and smiled. She'd even made a little joke about him getting a puppy for Robby.

Trace had gotten the puppy, a two-story colonial house, much of the furniture to go in it, and a swing

set for the backyard. He'd also gotten custody of
Robby. Madelyn had finally agreed. What he needed
now was a nanny. And Talia.

He called her from his office on Monday, but she
had just gotten a large to-go order. She said she was
sorry, but she was too busy to talk. He called her
again that night after he'd put Robby to bed. There
was no answer. That bothered him.

On Tuesday he made up his mind to go see her at
the shop, but something came up and he got buried
in work. He tried calling a couple more times that
night before it dawned that she was avoiding him.
That really bothered him.

Thursday night after reading a half dozen books to
Robby, he sat on his son's bed and critically examined his last meeting with Talia. She'd fidgeted a bit,
as if she'd been eager to get into her house. He'd had
to interrupt her in order to get her attention, he
recalled.

She'd reassured him, but her eyes . . . When
he'd told her he'd be in touch, she hadn't believed
him. Why not? For Pete's sake, he hadn't exactly
beat around the bush about his feelings. Of course
he wanted to see her again.

Idly tracing the pattern of a cartoon character on
Robby's bedspread, he frowned. It seemed he wasn't
getting answers from anyone. Philip was "out of
town," both Cynthia and his brother's secretary had
apologetically told him. He didn't return any of
Trace's calls, and Trace found Philip's silence damning. An insistent, ugly suspicion burned in his blood.

His thoughts turned to Talia again, who was never
far from his mind. He could almost smell her scent
and hear her laughter. Still, the lady had her doubts.
His hand stilled abruptly as he recalled how she'd
never fully committed herself to their relationship.

She'd said "I don't know," instead of "yes." He had assumed they would continue seeing each other after he got Robby settled in. But when he looked back on the last time he saw Talia, his gut clenched as he realized what her uneasiness and disbelief added up to.

She'd been saying good-bye.

He wondered what had been the deciding factor—the business with Philip or her misplaced concern over their different social worlds.

His heart sank, and for a moment the old loneliness seeped in. He'd won his son and lost his lady. Damned if it didn't hurt like hell.

But Trace wasn't the kind of man to accept such a defeat with good grace. The whole thing made him angry. It made him want to kick something or howl in frustration. Restraining himself, he carefully rose from Robby's bed and turned off the light. He closed the door behind him and walked down the hall to his bedroom.

He was angry with Talia for avoiding him. He was angry with Madelyn for taking her sweet time before giving him custody of Robby. He was angry with himself for picking such a bad time to fall for a hard-headed woman. At this point, he was angry that his room was painted blue.

A good old-fashioned display of temper would help. He eliminated his options the same way he'd slashed budgets his first day as CEO. He couldn't yell. He couldn't get drunk. He wouldn't kick the dog. Yet the frustration of wanting Talia and not having her burned a hole in his gut.

After stripping off his clothes, he stomped into the shower and swore for all he was worth. English, French, Italian curses; he wasn't choosy, just colorful. Until the hot water turned cold, he said things that would have singed a sailor's ears.

If nothing else, the swearing cleared his brain.

He made plans as he dried off with a fluffy beige towel. Talia wanted him. He just had to remind her of that. He smiled as he realized the LAM skating party was only two days away.

After Talia laced her roller skates, she knelt before Jason and tied his skates a little tighter. The crowd at the roller rink ranged in age from infancy to senior citizens. It appeared to Talia that the children were far less wobbly than the adults. As if to prove her point, a Barringer foreman barely broke his fall by grabbing her shoulder. Pushed off balance, she veered, but clutched the bench where Jason sat.

"Sorry, it's been a while," the man said sheepishly.

She smiled. "No problem." After watching the man hobble off, she turned to Jason. "You ready to learn how to skate backward, sport?"

"Yeah, let's go," Jason said eagerly. Talia noticed he even let her hold his hand. She figured that might last all of ten minutes. They moved out into the crowded rink and took a few practice turns around. Talia couldn't prevent herself from searching for Trace, but there was no sign of him yet. Perhaps that was for the best. She wouldn't be able to hide her excitement at seeing him. She'd missed him with an aching intensity over the past week.

Turning her attention back to Jason, she moved them to the edge of the rink and began to show him how to skate backward. She'd performed a couple of circles when someone plowed into her.

"Talia!" Robby shouted. "Where've you been?"

Talia landed on her bottom. She looked up at

Robby and couldn't stop a smile. The child moved at two speeds—the speed of light and dead to the world. "I've been working at my sub shop. Where've you been?" She got to her feet and gingerly rubbed her backside.

"I got a new house, and a Reptile Renegade bedspread, and a swing set, and a puppy," Robby blurted out.

"Wow, a Reptile Renegade bedspread?" Jason broke in.

"Yeah, it's really neat. Did you ever get your baby?"

"Yeah, it's a girl. But Dad told me Mom couldn't help it." Jason shrugged philosophically. "We named her Natalie. She's not that bad, and I get to hold her. I let Mom change her diapers, though. They're pretty messy."

Talia muffled her laugh.

Robby commiserated briefly with Jason, then turned back to Talia. "How come you haven't been to see us?"

That took her by surprise. She'd worked so hard to give Trace and Robby plenty of space. "Um, well, I guess I thought—"

"Talia's a busy lady," Trace finished for her as he rolled up beside the small group.

Her heart immediately beat faster.

"Hi," he said.

She felt devoured by his gaze, but knew her eyes were just as hungry for him. "Hi," she finally murmured.

The skaters continued around the rink and the music played on as they stared at each other, until Robby pulled at Trace's pants leg. "Dad," he said in exasperation, "how come you're not talking?"

Trace blinked, and a faint smile lifted the corners

of his lips. "I guess I've got something on my mind."

He gazed meaningfully at Talia's mouth, and she felt herself growing warm. She looked away and twisted an earring. She had a choice of six to fiddle with that night.

She cleared her throat. "Uh, I was just going to ask Jason if he wanted a soda. I'm feeling thirsty." Her mouth went as dry as the Sahara when Trace took her hand. "Would you and Robby like to join us?"

"I want to skate some more first," Jason said.

"I do too," Robby said.

"Okay, we'll be over on that bench if you need us," Trace said.

"Looks like it's just you and me," he added as they skated toward the drink stand.

"You and me and about a hundred other people," she said.

He chuckled. "A man's gotta have a dream."

When he made that kind of comment, Talia had the sensation of stepping off a high cliff. After Trace paid for their drinks, they carefully rolled to an empty bench.

She watched as Jason attempted to teach Robby how to skate backward. "So how's it going?"

Trace leaned back and stretched his arm across the top of the bench. "I've got a new house." He began to idly stroke her hair.

"Uh-huh," she said, loving the feel of his hand in her hair. "And a new puppy, swing set, and Reptile Renegade bedspread." It would have taken most people months to accomplish all that. Being a Barringer certainly had its advantages, she thought.

He gave her hair a little tug. "How did you know about the bedspread?"

She took a sip of her soda and grinned. "Robby told me, right after he knocked me down."

Trace grimaced. "Oh, sorry."

She opened her eyes wider. "Whatever for?"

He'd planned to start selling Talia on what a great package deal he and Robby were, but he didn't want her feeling overwhelmed by them. "Robby can be a little overexuberant at times."

"I think he's great. Look how hard he's trying to keep up with Jason." Talia watched the younger child take a nasty spill and set down her soda. "Oops, I better go check."

But Trace handed her his soda instead and stood. "No, you sit tight. I'm the parent."

She noticed the grim set of his mouth and frowned. What was his problem? she wondered. She had no intention of usurping his authority.

Trace gave Robby a hug and checked his knee. Before his dad had finished, Robby was pulling away, ready for more skating. Shaking his head, Trace returned to her side.

"Pretty resilient, isn't he?" Talia asked.

"Yeah. How are things at the shop?"

"Busy, and that's good."

He nodded. "I'm sorry I wasn't able to make the last LAM meeting, but—"

"Everyone understands," she interrupted. She noticed how he clenched and unclenched his fist, and felt concerned. "Is everything really okay with Robby?"

"Robby's fine. I've got custody of him, now."

"That's good."

He looked at her pointedly. "He's the least of my problems."

Puzzled, Talia wrinkled her brow. "Is it something at the office or with your family?"

He glanced away from her. "Neither."

When he began to tap his paper cup with his

forefinger, Talia knew something was very wrong. "Trace, look at you. You're fidgeting, and you never fidget. What is wrong?"

His jaw tightened. "I guess I don't like being dumped after a one-night stand."

She felt as if he'd punched her. "Dumped!"

His gaze fell over her like a warm, seeking hand. "What would you call it when you make love with a woman until you're crazy with the scent and taste of her and you repeatedly phone her, only to have her avoid you? What would you call it?"

A hard lump of emotion welled in her throat. There was anger in his rusty voice and hurt in his beautiful green eyes. If her goal had been to make the ending smoother between them, she'd failed miserably.

"I was trying to make it easier for you in case you had second thoughts." Her voice wavered. "I, uh, thought you might need some space."

"Space?" he repeated incredulously. "When the hell did I ask for space?"

Talia could suddenly imagine what Trace's employees felt like when they incurred his displeasure. She barely resisted the urge to squirm. "You didn't. But our time in Washington was rather . . ." Feeling uncomfortable, she turned away.

He caught her arm and pulled her back to face him. "Rather what? Exciting? Exhausting? Erotic?"

"Intense," she blurted out. Lord, she was botching this. Her thoughts were getting all jumbled up and the fact that Trace had both hands on her arms wasn't helping.

"We lead such different lives, Trace. I didn't know if your feelings would change once we got home."

"And what about your feelings?"

All of her barriers tumbled down at the hint of

uncertainty in his voice. "I've missed you," she whispered, "more than you could know."

"I doubt that," he muttered, and took a moment to absorb her confession. His heart lifted a little. "Then where have you been all the times I called you?"

He watched the color rise to her cheeks as she looked away.

"Yard work," she mumbled.

"Yard work?"

"Yes, yard work," she repeated testily. "I was upset after we came back from Camilia's. It was like withdrawal. I had to keep busy with something."

He chuckled and she glared at him.

"Crazy lady," he murmured, and bussed her forehead. "Do you realize how tormented I've been for the last week? When I go to bed, I remember everything about that night in Washington. The way you kiss, the way your skin feels, the sounds you make when you . . ." His voice trailed off as he remembered where they were.

Her eyes were full of the memories, too, the passion, the pleasure. She let out a shaky sigh and bit into her lower lip.

Trace withheld a groan and looked around. "Is there anywhere around here where I can kiss you?"

Talia heard the frustration in his voice. It matched her own. She shook her head. "Nowhere."

He cursed softly, but didn't release her yet. He looked at her silky hair, her expressive eyes, the earrings in her ears, and wanted her so much it made him crazy. He kept his voice low. "I've imagined you in my bed."

Talia sucked in a deep breath and tried to lighten the mood. She felt entirely too warm. "I hear anything's possible when you have a Reptile Renegade bedspread."

He laughed, and the sound landed in the pit of her stomach. He touched her hot cheek. "You're blushing."

Pulling away, she prayed for someone to drop a bucket of ice on her. "We've discussed this before. I don't blush. I'm not pale enough."

"It's not a pink blush," he said thoughtfully. "More of a dusty rose."

Indignantly, she faced him. "I don't blush. But if I did, it would be very rude of you to point it out."

He faked contrition. "I wouldn't want to be rude. How can I make it up to you?"

"Let's skate," she said briskly.

He took her hand, but his look was easily read. "Okay," he said. "For now."

# *Eight*

It wasn't smart.

Not smart at all to get so close to Trace and Robby. Not smart to eat dinner with them three nights the next week, or have Trace follow her back to her house after Robby had been tucked into bed. Not smart to ignore the fact that Kevin would be home within two weeks and she hadn't a prayer of explaining her feelings to him.

Not smart to ignore the differences that would always stand between her and Trace. It was easy to forget they were worlds apart when he held her in his arms or talked with her late at night. But when she was away from him, she remembered he was far more educated, sophisticated, and wealthy than she could ever hope to be. Than she ever wanted to be, for that matter.

Talia sighed and dismissed her disturbing thoughts. She glanced at her alarm clock, then at Trace, and a smile found its way to her lips.

He was sprawled in naked contentment amid her cotton sheets. He was also sleeping. She couldn't help but admire him. She'd done that quite a bit lately, in and out of bed.

He was such an attentive father, listening to Robby's chatter, laughing with his son, encouraging Talia to join in. She never felt excluded. It seemed both of them were always touching her. Trace would slide his hand around her waist or touch her hair. Robby would grab her hand and drag her off to see something or give her a wet kiss.

It was dangerous. It made her hope and dream.

But Talia was too happy to upset the applecart. She knew that time would come without any help from her. She'd deal with it then. Right now she needed to wake Sleeping Beauty and send him home. By mutual agreement, he never stayed overnight. He'd hired a wonderful live-in nanny for Robby, but he needed to be there in case of nightmares.

She smoothed his eyebrows and ran his fingers through his love-mussed hair. "Trace," she said softly, "it's time to get up."

Grudgingly, he opened one eye. "It can't be time. I just got here."

"It's eleven-thirty. Time for all good CEOs to be in their own bed."

He closed his eye again, but a sexy grin teased the corners of his mouth. "'Good' is a rather bland term, wouldn't you say?" He snatched her hand and placed it on his chest.

Dirty pool, Talia thought. Trace knew she was endlessly fascinated with his chest. Of its own accord, her hand wandered over it, combing through the dusting of brown hair and playing with his nipples.

Catching herself, she pushed away and sat up. She automatically pulled the sheet to her, leaving

Trace in a rather exposed position, which he ignored. She, however, could not.

"You're always kicking me out of bed, Talia," he said as he opened his eyes and raised himself to his elbows.

"You need to get back to Robby," she reminded him.

He frowned. "I know, but do you have to be so damned enthusiastic about it?"

She smiled, managing not to laugh. "I guess I could weep and pitch a fit every night. Would that help?"

He plucked at the sheet, then looked up at her, his expression serious. "No, but it would be nice if I knew you wanted me to stay."

Her breath caught. Trace could do that to her with just a look, yet this time he did it with words. She leaned over him and touched his chest. "You must know that I want you to stay."

He rubbed his face into her palm. "You never say it."

She almost protested, then realized it was true. Trace was always praising her, but she was too awestruck or shy to tell him how she felt. A tinge of guilt sneaked in when she saw how she'd made him suffer. Another step closer, she thought, and decided it was time.

"I want you, Trace. It feels like I want you all the time. The bed is cold and lonely when you leave. There are times in the middle of the night when I have to force myself not to phone you just to hear your voice."

Chagrin swept over her. "Do you know how many orders I've messed up thinking about you instead of work?"

"Salami instead of turkey?" he asked, looking very pleased. He pulled her closer and kissed her palm.

"Something like that." Sobering, she bared a little more of her soul. "I want you, Trace, like I've never wanted anybody else."

She was flat on her back with his mouth pressed to hers before she could take a breath. The kiss was full of passion, charged with emotion, demanding her response. She gave it in full measure.

Finally Trace pulled back and looked at her for a long moment. He could drown in her soft brown eyes, lose his mind when she smiled. He touched the mole above her mouth, then ran his hand to the three gold beads in her ear.

"The next time you feel like calling me in the middle of the night, do it," he said as his hands grew more restless. He stroked her hair and cheek, then extended the caress to her neck and shoulders, gorging himself with the satiny texture of her skin.

Drawing circles around her breasts, he watched her nipples pucker before he touched them. Her breathing quickened, and his mouth went dry the way it always did.

"Trace," she whispered huskily.

Leaning down, he took one rosy bud into his mouth and suckled. Her trembling tightened his already hard body. Suddenly, he knew that seeing Talia for a few hours here and there wouldn't be enough. The implication of that knowledge could have scared him, but need superseded fear. In time, they would have to deal with what was happening to them. Right now they had a few stolen moments, and he'd give her everything he could.

"We've got to make this bed so hot," he murmured, "it stays warm until morning. I can't have you getting cold."

She smiled, and his heart turned over. "We haven't got long," she said.

He flicked his tongue over her other nipple. "You want to help?"

She smoothed her fingers down his chest, hovering at his belly button while he shifted to accommodate her. She gently wrapped her hand around his aching fullness.

"What do you think?" she asked as she began to stroke him.

Trace just groaned.

"She's gorgeous, Gina," Talia said to her friend the next day. Gina had brought her baby daughter to the shop to show her off. Talia cooed at the wide-eyed infant, "What does Don think of her?"

"He's in love," Gina said smugly. "All Natalie has to do is blow a few bubbles or bat those baby blues and he gets all misty-eyed."

Talia shook her head at the notion of Don getting weepy over a baby. Still, when she looked at Natalie, she felt a tug at her heartstrings herself. For a fleeting moment, she wondered what her baby would look like if Trace was the father.

The jingling of the bell at the door diverted her attention. Freddie swept in and handed her a package from the Barringer complex. "Thank you," she called as he raced back out the door. Freddie had acted much more reserved around her since that incident with Trace over a month ago.

"Boring business stuff?" Gina asked, shifting her little burden to get a better look.

"I don't know," Talia murmured as she tore off the brown wrapping paper. "I've never gotten anything from them before."

She opened the box. It took her a moment to identify the green stuffed animal, then she laughed out loud.

"What is it? Let me see," Gina said.

Talia laughed again and held up the green creature.

"A Reptile Renegade," Gina said, a baffled expression on her face. "Who in the world would send you a Reptile? And why?"

Talia saw the note in the bottom of the box and read it silently.

> Hope you were still warm this morning. I was. Bill me for any mistakes you make on your orders today.
>
> Trace

"He couldn't afford it," she murmured, smiling.

"Couldn't afford what?" Gina asked. "Talia, you're acting very strange."

"He couldn't afford all the mistakes I'll make today." She folded the note and tucked it into her pocket. When a customer came through the door, Gina got distracted with displaying her new little girl. Natalie soon began to fuss, though, forcing Gina to wave a harried good-bye while Talia waited on the customer.

Afterward, as she dropped *The Marriage of Figaro* into the cassette player, Talia's happy mood faded when she thought of the dinner date that evening with Trace and some out-of-town business associates. Knowing she'd feel uncomfortable, she'd tried to beg off. It was difficult to refuse Trace, though. She wanted to make the right impression on his colleagues and friends, wanted to be an asset to him. Still, she had serious doubts about her ability.

Dinner conversation at the four-star restaurant that night went straight over her head. After Trace's business associates Hal and David bemoaned the unstable stock market, their wives, Deirdre and Mary, chatted about trips to Europe. The closest Talia had been to Europe was a local European theme amusement park.

Her hands went clammy at the array of sterling silverware on the table. She saved herself from embarrassment by watching which fork the others used first. But with her concentration fixed on the silverware, she nearly knocked over her wineglass.

When talk turned to baseball, she relaxed marginally and even joined in. Having a brother obsessed with the Red Sox paid off. Trace squeezed her hand, and the gesture warmed her to her toes.

The warm feeling would have lasted the rest of the evening if she hadn't overheard Deirdre and Mary in the powder room.

"Did you notice her nails?" Deirdre asked. "My mother always said the mark of a true lady lies in how she grooms her hands."

Standing just outside the washroom area, Talia looked at her hands and saw fingernails cut to a neat, serviceable length and calluses on her palms.

"I didn't notice her nails," Mary said. "I was too busy admiring her hair."

"Her dress is definitely off the rack," Deirdre pointed out.

Talia stiffened, glancing down at the cream-colored dress she'd been so proud of. Deidre's words hit her so hard, she wondered if she was going to be sick. Trace had probably never been with a woman who'd worn anything but designer originals, she realized. Distantly, she heard the sound of paper towels being torn from a dispenser.

"Yes," Mary said. "But Trace sure looks happy."

Blinking away sudden, angry tears, Talia fled back to the table, wishing she'd left the washroom earlier. The women's comments left her feeling self-conscious and confused.

Trace noticed her subdued mood on the drive home and finally dragged the incident from her.

His mouth tightened. "Deirdre's a bitch. We won't see them again."

"But they're your friends. You can't cut them off just because Deirdre made an idle comment about my dress."

"I most certainly can. We don't need those kind of people cluttering up our life."

Talia sighed. She wondered how many more friends Trace would have to give up because of his relationship with her. The thought depressed her.

When she remained quiet, he glanced at her. "You're not really going to let someone like Deirdre get to you, are you? Ignore her. I do."

"But they're your friends."

"So are Mary and David. What did Mary say?"

"She said you sure looked happy," Talia said in a small voice.

Trace relaxed. "That's because I am happy." He reached across the seat to capture her hand. "And I'm happy because of you. Remember that."

She'd be hard-pressed to forget it, Talia thought later, after the lingering emotional kiss they shared. The way he looked at her when he reluctantly said good night would stay with her for a long time. But try as she might, she couldn't completely erase the doubts in the back of her mind.

The following evening Trace's nanny took the night off for her weekly bridge game, so Talia fixed lasagna for the three of them at Trace's house.

After the meal Trace leaned back in his chair and sighed in contentment. "I thought you said you couldn't cook Italian food."

"No," she corrected him as she cleared the table. "I said Kevin was the lasagna cooker in our family. And he is. I *can* make Italian food. I just usually don't feel like taking the time. Between my mother being sick and my cooking, Kevin got more than his share of sandwiches." She chuckled. "I think desperation drove him to learn how to cook."

Trace picked up Robby's plate and followed her into the kitchen. "When do I get to meet him?"

She halted her scraping for a moment then continued. "He'll probably be home in a week or so. Where did Robby go?"

Trace noticed the swift change in subject, but didn't comment. "He's watching a cartoon on TV. Does Kevin know about us?"

Her back stiffened. She turned the water on full force. "I haven't really talked to him that much lately. I think he was going to stop off at some friends in New York after camping. I'm just about finished here. Would you like some coffee?"

She looked like a high-speed windup doll, Trace mused, as she slid the dishes into the dishwasher. He didn't want the tension between them, not yet, so he let it pass and poured the coffee.

She glanced up. "I would have gotten it."

"It's okay," he said, and handed her a cup. "You've done everything else. Let's go into the den."

They walked through the hall to the comfortable room. She heard the sound of the TV from the living room farther down the hall. Green loungers and a striped sofa stocked with plump pillows were arranged in a cozy formation on the plush beige carpet. Walnut end tables coordinated with the paneling.

"I love this room," she murmured, taking a seat on the sofa.

Trace sat beside her and touched the sleeve of her lightweight sweater. "Tomato sauce."

She rolled her eyes. "That's the second reason I hardly ever make lasagna." She plucked at the red spot, then gave up. "I'm as bad as Robby."

Trace remembered his orange-faced son and shook his head. "Not quite as bad. But it reminds me of when you ran your bike into that guy who was about to smash my head. What happened to you? It seemed like you were there one second and gone the next."

"I didn't want anyone to recognize me." When she saw his frown of confusion, she set her coffee aside and explained. "I wasn't supposed to be riding my bike at night. I wasn't supposed to be riding through town, either, but since I was late for my curfew, I took a shortcut from the lake."

"I remember your hair was wet."

She nodded. "I stayed at the lake too long. It was the only place I really felt free back then. I was hoping I could get out of being grounded. My mother took one look at my knees and silently cleaned them up. She was so quiet, I wished she'd yell." Her mouth quirked into a half smile. "I got my wish a minute later. Half of it was in Italian, so I didn't understand a lot. But she converted to English long enough to tell me I was grounded for a month."

Trace squeezed her shoulder. "I didn't get grounded. I just got a lecture from my mother about how intelligent people use their brains and not their fists. Then she looked at my swollen eye, burst into tears, gave me a steak, and turned me over to my father." Trace chuckled. "He wanted a blow-by-blow description. Then he said he agreed with my mother, but that there are times when a man has to fight. He said he was proud of me and warned me that the eye was going to hurt like hell." He looked at Talia. "He was right."

She laughed. "Kevin very generously offered to ride my bike for me while my knees were recovering. He said he wouldn't want the bike to get rusty from lack of use."

Trace grinned. "The next morning at breakfast, Valerie said I looked like I belonged in a horror movie. She offered to take my picture and send it to Hollywood."

They both laughed. Talia thought of the shy blonde teenage girl she'd met only a few times. "What is she doing now?"

"She lives in England," Trace said. "She went to a finishing school about—"

"Six years ago," Talia said.

He hesitated, then nodded. "Yes. Valerie lived with our aunt Patrice until Patrice died. We all thought she would move back then, but she didn't. She's only been home two or three times in the last six years." And she had treated the whole family distantly, he thought, frowning.

"I'd chase Kevin down and visit him myself if he pulled something like that. We're too close."

"I tried," Trace said. "But every time I called her, she said she was busy. I thought she needed some space."

It was on the tip of Talia's tongue to say that something monumental must have happened for Valerie to leave, but she kept her mouth shut.

The truth will out, she told herself. But she wondered what would happen when it did. Trace loved his family too much to take this kind of thing lightly. And even though she understood family loyalty, it grated on her that he was still confident there'd been a terrible misunderstanding.

The ticking of the clock made her think of how soon Kevin would come home. Things could blow up in her face then. Apprehension and a touch of panic raced through her. She wasn't ready to let Trace go. Even for Kevin. But she wouldn't want to hurt Kevin.

She slammed the door on her unwelcome thoughts, and remembered how delighted she'd been with the gift she'd received from Trace the day before. "You know, I never thanked you."

His face lost the hard edge of concentration. He looked at her and smiled. "For what?"

She could tell by his eyes that he knew what. And he looked entirely too self-satisfied for her taste. "For the dozen red roses you sent me," she said with wide-eyed innocence. "There was no card, but I knew they were from you."

She reached over and placed a kiss on his suddenly tight jaw. "It was so thoughtful, Trace," she gushed, "even if it wasn't very imaginative."

"Imaginative! I didn't send you roses. I sent you—" He broke off when he saw the gleam in her eye. "You witch. I was sitting here trying to figure out who was moving in on you."

He hauled her onto his lap. "That wasn't very nice, Talia," he said in a low, threatening voice.

A chill ran down her spine, but she laughed anyway. "Oh no. This doesn't mean I'm going to have trouble getting you to pay your bill, does it?"

"Bill?" he asked, trying desperately to keep up with her.

"I messed up twenty-six dollars and fourteen cents' worth of subs yesterday because of you."

He gave her that devastating smile that always took her breath. "Twenty-six fourteen," he said, playing with the hoop earring in her ear. "How do you want your payment?"

Heat rushed through her at the possessive expression in his gaze. She said the only thing that came to her mind and felt a little shocked at her brazenness. "Any way you want to give it."

His eyes turned dark emerald, and he brought her face closer with commanding hands. She instinctively clung to his shoulders, needing the anchor. She knew without a doubt who was in control of this situation, because it sure wasn't her. Her heart was beating a mile a minute, and the cloudiness in her mind increased with each idle stroke of his finger against her ear.

He brought her lips to his and turned her head to the side. When he lightly flicked his tongue against her lips, she sighed. He caught the puff of breath and slid his tongue inside her mouth, along the edge of her teeth. His hands remained curled around her head, caressing and stroking her hair.

She fell against him and moaned at the sensation of her aching breasts against his solid chest. His scent wove its way around her, drawing her deeper, deeper . . .

"Does this mean you're getting married?" a young voice asked.

Talia ripped her mouth from Trace's and looked around with dazed eyes. One of Trace's hands was still in her hair, and when she turned her head, he accidentally pulled her hair.

"Ouch!" The unexpected pain brought tears to her eyes.

"Just a minute," he muttered, and concentrated on the task of untangling her hair from his fingers.

Under Robby's watchful gaze, she felt like a teenager caught necking. Without forethought, she shifted.

Trace ground his teeth and said under his breath, "If you have one ounce of mercy, you'll be still."

When she realized what he was referring to, her face flamed. She knew it, because Robby said with childish candor, "Your face is red."

Trace chuckled.

Talia scrambled off his lap. Her hair could grow back, she told herself, and took a deep breath. "Tell me about the cartoon you watched, Robby."

Robby looked puzzled, then shrugged as if he was accustomed to adults acting strangely. "It was about a dog," he began.

Dodging meaningful glances from Trace, Talia listened and asked a few questions, then said it was time for her to go. Robby gave her a hug and kiss.

Trace followed her out to her car and took her hand. She felt sheepish. "Sorry I overreacted."

He smiled and shook his head. "That's okay. For a moment there, I forgot where I was too." He kissed her and squeezed her hand. "See you tomorrow?"

She felt soothed by the fondness in his eyes and the touch of his hand. The fire was always there, but he could control it. The knowledge made her feel secure. "Tomorrow," she promised, and got into her car.

But Kevin arrived the next day with Professor David Shelton in tow. Talia concealed her disappointment, though not her surprise. Then she felt so guilty over feeling disappointed, she agreed to attend Lung Awareness Night with David and Kevin at Gus's Bar the next night.

Trace called just as the three of them were finishing dinner. "Do you want me to come over to your house," he asked, "or do you want to come over here?"

"Umm," she began, looking at Kevin and David.

Trace's low laugh brought a flutter to her stomach. "After last night, I thought it might be a good idea if we had some time alone."

"I—I don't think I'm going to be able to make it tonight. You see, Kevin came home."

"Oh." Trace quickly rearranged his plans. "I've been wanting to meet him. I could come over and leave early."

"Well," she said, and he heard the nervousness in her voice, "Kevin kind of brought someone with him for the weekend."

Trace frowned. He knew Talia was uneasy about him meeting Kevin, but she sounded downright panicky now. "You don't want me to meet him," he said.

"It's not that. At least not totally." She breathed a sigh of relief as her brother and David headed for the den.

The silence drew out for Trace. He could practically see her twisting the telephone cord. "Talia," he prompted.

"They left for a minute. Kevin did this one other time a couple of years ago. He's got this crazy idea that he needs to provide me with . . . men." Her words came out in a jerky rush. "I don't know why. Anyway, he brought home this calculus professor— his name's David—for the weekend, and they want me to take them to Gus's tomorrow night."

Trace was trying to absorb it with a cool, logical mind. But he got hung up about halfway through on the word "men." "Men?" he repeated, his voice tight. "Exactly what does Kevin want this David"—he said the name with distaste—"man to do with you?"

"Well, Kevin doesn't think small. He's probably hoping for a marriage proposal within three months." Her choked laugh didn't help Trace one bit. "I think my little brother fantasizes about me selling the sub shop and leaving Barringer for good. Then he wouldn't ever have to come back."

Trace could have sworn his heart stopped. "Talia—"

"Listen, I gotta go," she said quickly, and he heard male voices in the background. "I'll talk to you in a few days, Trace. Sorry," she whispered, and hung up.

He hesitated for a second, then replaced the receiver. Trace prided himself on being a rational, intelligent man, not given to displays of nerves.

So why were his hands sweating?

The next evening as Talia was getting ready for their outing, Kevin came into her bedroom and leaned against the doorjamb. She glanced at him in the mirror and felt her heart swell with pride. He'd turned out well, resembling their big Irish father. With his dark hair, vivid blue eyes, and broad shoulders, he turned many female heads. But Kevin's interest wasn't easily captured. And his heart . . . Well, his heart might never trust again. She despaired over that and sighed.

"Heavy thoughts?" he asked.

"Not really," she said. "I was just thinking how much you look like Daddy."

Kevin shrugged. It was a common enough comment, but he barely remembered his father. "What do you think of David?"

She hesitated. "He's very nice, very . . . intelligent." Talia enjoyed a challenging intellectual discussion as much as the next person. But she felt as if she'd been caught in a calculus time warp since David had arrived.

Kevin sighed in understanding. "He really likes calculus."

"I guess that's why he teaches it," she said tactfully.

"And teaches it," Kevin added, smiling.

"And teaches it," she said, and they both laughed.

"How'd you lure him down here, anyway?" Talia asked as she gave Kevin a hug.

"I showed him your picture."

"And he was so impressed, he had to come down here?" she asked with heavy irony.

"Well, he's never been south of the Mason-Dixon Line."

She nodded in understanding.

"I also promised to help him out with tutoring freshmen next year."

She pushed him aside in mock affront. "You had to bribe him? Give it up, Kevin. I'll pick my own man."

"How are you gonna pick one if you never go out? I think you missed a crucial stage in your development. It's preventing you from forming a relationship with a man."

She averted her eyes. If Kevin only knew. She was sinking like a stone in deep water when it came to Trace. "I go out," she argued, then switched the subject. "Crucial stage in my development? Did you take Psychology this semester?"

He grinned.

Shaking her head, she grabbed his arm and pulled him to the door. "C'mon, let's show David a genuine redneck bar."

• • •

A party atmosphere filled the small bar. The pa-
trons wore denim and leather and swilled beer. A live
band played songs about cheating hearts and love
gone wrong. The only thing missing was smoke. A
sign posted at the door threatened anyone who
dared to light a cigarette that they would be shot on
sight.

So far there'd been three casualties.

Gus, the owner, had drawn his water pistol on the
now damp souls who'd forgotten the night's special
rule. He'd then sympathetically offered bubble gum
cigars. Gus had his own wad of bubble gum taking
the place of his usual cigarette.

Talia noticed Kevin's gaze hovering on a blonde
who kept walking past their table. "See anyone you
want to dance with?"

Kevin took a drink of his beer and gave his sister a
"mind your own business" look.

"I think her name is Audrey," Talia continued.

"Thank you," he said gravely, then turned to
David, who'd given up on his discussion of statistics
due to the loud noise.

"David, I think Talia wants to dance. She's just too
shy to say so."

"Would you care to dance, Talia?" David asked
immediately, then paused to listen. "I believe this
number is done in three-quarter time."

Talia blinked. Mathematics in music. She couldn't
think of a thing to say, so she took the hand David
offered and stood. She looked back at Kevin and
mouthed the word "Shy!"

Kevin laughed.

David led her in a surprisingly smooth shuffle. She
asked him about his family and had to shout in his

ear. By the end of the song they were both laughing. She was about to suggest they return to their table, when the band jumped into a lively tune.

David cut loose and bopped her around the dance floor with spins and even a few dips.

"You look surprised," he yelled in her ear.

"I am," she said breathlessly, and smiled. Her brother's friend might have an obsession for numbers, but he was very nice. If it weren't for Trace, maybe she could work up more enthusiasm for another man. David was tall with stylishly cut brown hair. And his eyes were hazel flecked with gold.

His hold on her was firm, but deferential. She preferred that. The only man she wanted embracing her as if he'd never let go was Trace. The man who'd opened her up to her own femininity and made her like it.

It was useless, she realized. Here she was, her head bent toward the floor in a dip with David's face inches from hers, close enough to kiss.

It could have been a romantic moment, but her primary concern was the crick in her neck.

# *Nine*

---

Trace entered the packed tavern and glanced around. It would have been wiser to stay at home, but something had driven him to the bar that night. More like someone. Someone Italian with dark hair, wide brown eyes, and a smile that drove him wild.

After making his way to the bar, he ordered a Scotch. There weren't any seats, so he remained standing and gave a brief nod to one of his foremen. Lots of cowboy hats tonight, he noticed.

His gaze traveled to the wooden dance floor. People had moved aside in honor of a couple in the center. An unfamiliar man held the woman in a deep dip. Her long hair swung close to the floor as she held tight to her partner's shoulders. Trace stared hard, then his heart slipped to his feet as he recognized Talia.

A fist of anger formed in his belly. His first instinct was to rush across the floor and rip Talia from the man's arms. But the voices around him penetrated the haze of anger, reminding him that this was a public place. If he did what he wanted to that guy, there would be witnesses. He would be put away for life.

He took a long swallow of Scotch and looked away. His glance landed on a nearby table. Only one person occupied it, and there was something familiar about the man. Trace stared at him long enough for the guy to feel it and return the stare.

Remembering the picture in Talia's living room, Trace walked toward the man. It was Kevin, he realized. And with Talia entertaining the professor, it was the perfect time for him to meet her brother.

"Would you mind if I sit here for a minute?" he asked.

"Sorry, my sister and—"

"—your professor friend from M.I.T. are using these seats," Trace finished, and watched faint surprise cross Kevin's face.

Kevin met his gaze, then turned away. "Yeah."

A hard case, Trace thought, but sat down anyway. "Talia's told me a lot about you. I've been looking forward to meeting you."

Kevin took a swallow of beer, but still didn't look at Trace.

"I'm Trace Barringer."

"I know."

Trace raised an eyebrow. "How?"

Kevin's mouth firmed. "Your sister, she's got the same green eyes."

"I haven't seen her much lately."

"Join the club," Kevin said, and finally looked at Trace.

It was then that Trace saw he was dealing with a man, not a college boy. Kevin had a man's eyes. If what Talia said was true, his abrupt entrance into manhood had been horrendous. If what Talia said was true, Philip was responsible. But even though that issue couldn't be settled in Gus's bar that night, others could.

Trace changed the subject. "How'd you end up with blue eyes?"

Kevin shrugged. "They say I look like my dad."

They say. Trace caught the unspoken. Kevin had never known his dad.

"I hear you've got a scholarship," he said, and took another drink of Scotch.

Kevin set his own drink down and turned to Trace. His young face was a study of barely controlled impatience. "What do you want?"

Trace didn't pause one second. "Talia."

A spark flared in Kevin's eyes, and his hand tensed around his glass. "Forget it."

Trace just shook his head.

"She wouldn't look twice at a Barringer."

Trace heard the bitterness, saw the pain behind the words. Kevin felt betrayed. "I think she said something like that about a month ago."

Kevin relaxed his grip on his glass and nodded.

Trace knew he was going to have to hurt Kevin even more and wasn't happy about it. Still, it had to be done if Talia and he were going to move ahead. "Talia's done a lot more than look twice at me since then."

Kevin's eyes narrowed dangerously. "You'd damn well better watch what you say about my sister."

"I could say a lot more," Trace continued calmly. "You see, I'm in love with her." He smiled grimly to himself. He hadn't even said the words to Talia. "And I think she feels the same way about me."

"You're crazy. If you were important to Talia, she would have told me. Our family isn't like yours. We don't keep secrets from each other."

Trace sucked in a hard breath. That last statement

was better than a poison-tipped arrow. He had wondered if the fact that Talia wanted to keep their relationship secret meant he'd misinterpreted her feelings.

"And you're a Barringer." Kevin practically spat out the name.

Fierce family loyalty warred with regret over Kevin's tragic experience. "My name is Trace, not Philip."

Kevin shrugged. "Same difference."

The match lit on Trace's temper. A hundred years ago, he and Kevin could have battled this out in a much more satisfying manner. Trace leaned forward across the table. This fight was going to get dirtier before it got resolved. "You've got Talia fooled."

Kevin sat up straighter.

"She's proud of you," Trace continued. "She brags about you so much, I'd never have thought you were so narrow-minded. Especially if you were ever in love with my sister. It takes a strong man to overcome what you've been through." He gave Kevin an appraising glance. "Maybe Talia overestimated you."

Kevin gritted his teeth. "You bastard."

Trace ignored the insult, seeing the shaken confidence beneath Kevin's manner. "She's afraid of what you'll think. You're important to her."

"And I suppose you expect me to turn my head," Kevin said tightly.

"No. I'd just like you not to sabotage our relationship. I want to make Talia happy."

"I don't think you can."

"But I do. I'm willing to make amends with you. I can't make you accept our relationship, but I won't let anyone stand in our way. She's too important to me."

The band slid into a slow lover's tune. Looking toward the dance floor, Trace saw the professor pull

Talia closer. He was aware that Kevin was watching him. The hostility was still there, warring with something else he couldn't read.

He turned back to Kevin. "I'm a tolerant man, Kevin. But if you bring any more men home for Talia, I might have to do something rash."

Not waiting for a response, he stood and walked over to the dancing couple. "Excuse me," he said with what he thought was remarkable control, considering how close the man's hands were to Talia's hips. "I'm cutting in."

David looked up in surprise, stopping mid-step. Trace used the moment to pull Talia into his arms and away from David.

Talia naturally fit her body to Trace's while her mind came to an abrupt halt. She stared up at him. "What are you doing here?"

"Looking out for my interests." He said the words lightly, but his jaw was clenched and his hands held her tight. "I had a little chat with Kevin." And he'd gotten mixed results at best. He suspected Talia wasn't going to be happy.

"You told him about us," she said accusingly.

"I knew it would be too hard for you to tell him. It had to be done."

"You should have waited." Talia looked over Trace's shoulder, desperately seeking Kevin. Oh, he must be so hurt, she thought. She caught her brother's gaze and searched for some sign of his feelings. His face was set in a dark, forbidding frown. Her heart dropped to her knees. "He's hurt and angry." She tried to work free, but Trace held her firmly.

"He'll get over it. He's got to think it through." Trace felt a sick knot of desperation in his gut, knowing that if she pulled away from him, it would slice him in half.

She remained stiffly in his arms, torn between running to Kevin and staying with Trace. Still, after just one day, she'd missed Trace so much, she ached. She watched Kevin deliberately turn away and speak to David, then the two men left the bar. "Maybe I should go too," she whispered around a throat swollen with unshed tears.

"What will you tell him, Talia? That there's nothing between us?"

She closed her eyes. "No. I'd have to tell him the truth."

The tension inside Trace eased. "That's what I did. He deserved to know."

"I know, but it hurt him. It hurt him terribly."

"It's a shock right now. You need to give him time to get used to the idea."

She looked at him. "Do you really think so?"

Lord knows, he hoped so. Instinct told him that Kevin would ultimately be fair. "It might take some time, but I think he'll come around."

She swiped at the dampness around her eyes. "You're right. He had to be told and it would have been too hard for me to do it." She touched his cheek. "I've missed you."

The simple words made his heart swell. He tucked her head beneath his chin and wrapped his arms around her. "Did anyone ever tell you you're hell on a man's nervous system? When I first came in here I was thinking about murdering your professor."

Jealousy. Talia identified the emotion easily. And she cared too much for Trace to cause him any pain. "He's a good dancer," she said, and felt Trace stiffen. Pulling back a little, she gazed into his eyes. "But the whole time I was in his arms I kept wishing it was you."

A fierce expression swept over his face. "I *need* to be alone with you."

She shook her head. "I do too. But I've got company and you've got Robby."

His brows drew together in a frown, then smoothed out. "I know where to go," he said, and drew her closer. "But for right now, guardian angel, just dance with me."

Her heart soaring at the simple request, she folded herself closer to him, feeling her apprehensions melt away.

And dance they did, setting off sparks with their slow movements. She would always remember this song, not for the words, but for the way Trace held her. The way he smelled and felt would be imprinted on her mind with this melody in the background. His lips caressed her hair while she rested her cheek against his shoulder, one hand over his heart. Denim rubbed against denim as their thighs pressed close.

Trace inhaled deeply and squeezed her hips. "You know," he murmured in her ear, "you never have told me what kind of perfume you wear."

In spite of the fire that he was building within her, she smiled. "The English translation is—"

He shifted positions, fitting her more snugly into the cradle of his thighs. Her breath caught as he lightly pushed his erection against her.

Her knees lost their starch, and she gripped his shoulders. He grinned that maddening smile. He could see what he was doing to her.

After all this time, though, she was determined to tell him now. Call it retribution for how easily he seduced her. Call it frustration. Call it whatever. She stretched up on her toes and said in a husky voice timeless with feminine lure, "Ecstasy. It's called Ecstasy."

His hands wrapped around her arms like steel bands. "We're in public and you're pushing it."

"You asked," she pointed out, then continued, improvising as she went. "The exact translation, I believe, is 'ecstatic soaring into the heavens.'"

He was barely moving, but she could see his pulse pound in his temple. His face was flushed, his lips tight.

She was tired of dancing. Edgy, breathless, needy. She watched him battle for control, wanting him to lose it as she had so many times. Had the tables turned? If so, why was she having a hard time forming coherent thoughts?

"How high do you want to go, Trace?" she asked.

His gaze was like a hot flame. "As high as we can, Talia," he replied in a rough voice.

It awed her that they were so responsive to each other. They needed to be together, but it was more than just physical. It came from deep within as if their hearts, their very souls, longed to couple. The only choice was the full merging of their bodies.

He stared at her lips with such intensity, she would swear she'd been kissed. Taking her hand, he stepped away from her. "Are you ready?"

She nodded.

After guiding her from the bar, he folded her into his Corvette and started up the engine. He took time out for a kiss that made them both a little crazy, then slammed the car into gear.

Talia desperately wanted to touch him. She could hardly bear the distance between them.

"Hold on," he said, sensing her frustration, and placed her hand on his hard thigh. They hit the only two red lights in town. Trace used the delays for more kisses, each time letting his hands drift over her shoulders, breasts, and hips before he pulled away. Each time the low tense ache inside her tightened.

She studied his face in the brief gleam of oncoming headlights. His expression was intense, his eyes dark. His muscles bunched beneath her hand. She stretched against the confining seatbelt and brushed her open mouth on his neck. He exhaled a long ragged breath, but didn't move away.

"I can't get close enough," she murmured.

"You will," he promised, shifting into fourth. "Touch me."

"I am," she said, damning time because it seemed to stand still.

He shook his head and led her hand to his heat. Holding her palm over his hard arousal, he squeezed, then returned his own shaking hand to the steering wheel. The feel of his need against her made her dizzy. She stroked, mindless of where they were. Her breathing quickened with his. Vaguely, she noticed the car take a sharp turn, then another.

Trace wrenched the 'Vette to a stop, then hauled Talia to the door of the Barringer cottage. It was pitch-black, and he cursed the seconds it took to find the key.

She leaned against him and raced through the door with as much urgency as he. Closing the door with his foot, he immediately turned to her, kissing her. She pulled at his shirt. He pulled at hers, losing a few buttons on the oak floor in the process.

"This is crazy," he murmured against her neck, then swept his mouth to her breast.

She cried out, and he immediately stepped away. "Am I hurting you?"

"No," she said, and unbuckled his belt with trembling hands. "Trace, I just want you so badly. Don't make me wait."

Even in the dark, she saw his nostrils flare and his eyes light like a roaring blaze. The fire swept her into its center, making her aware of only him.

He took her mouth and shoved her jeans down her weak legs. She clung to him while he made short work of his own jeans and briefs. His hands tested the heat of her skin and the dewy moistness between her thighs. He stroked her until a husky whimper escaped her throat.

Pulling away for a moment, he protected them, then lifted her. "I could take you to bed, but I swear I don't think I can make it that far."

He pushed her against the wall. She instinctively swung her legs around his hips, and he plunged into her.

Hushed whispers accompanied the slide of slick skin against slick skin. It took only a few thrusts before the coil inside Talia exploded, and she swept Trace with her into a swirling vortex of sensation.

They were gasping for air when they came back down. His mouth puffed breaths against her neck, then she thought she heard a weak chuckle.

"Are the walls still standing?" he asked.

"Don't ask me. I'll not seeing straight yet."

The next chuckle sounded a little stronger. He shifted.

"If you set me down, I'll fall," she warned. "My legs are like jelly."

"Don't worry," he assured her, and shuffled to the living room. They fell to the sofa, legs entwined, arms still wrapped around each other.

Trace groaned and covered his face with his hand. "Lord, woman, what you do to me."

Suddenly remembering the last time she'd been in the cottage, Talia began to laugh.

He pulled his hand from his face and looked at her quizzically. "What?"

"I'm just remembering something you said the last time I was here." Another laugh escaped. "I told you I thought I'd be safer on my feet."

He smiled and lifted her onto his chest. "And I told you that someone had neglected your education." He twisted a strand of her hair. "I think I'm the one who got an education tonight. Two days without you and I'm not quite sane anymore." His face turned serious. "Did I hurt you?"

His concern touched her deep inside. It was warm and comforting to her heart and just as important, she found, as the blazing desire between them. "No," she said, and spotted teeth marks on his shoulder. She smoothed her finger over them. "But I'm worried, Trace. Was I too rough with you?"

She gazed at him with such apprehension, he had to laugh. He proceeded, with tenderness and patience, to reassure her.

Much later, Talia lay in his arms, hovering at the edge of sleep. The sound of a car door slamming penetrated their lazy intimacy. She tensed.

"What's wrong?" Trace asked, waking up.

"I thought I heard—"

There was a knock at the door.

"Who is it?" she whispered, then remembered her state of undress. "Where are my clothes?"

"Just a minute," Trace called. "Wait here," he said in a softer voice to her, "and I'll get your clothes."

After gathering the strewn clothing in the foyer and returning to her, he put his jeans and shirt on in record time. "Who is it?" she asked again.

"Philip."

"Philip!" She fumbled with buttons that didn't want to match up with their holes. "Where should I go?"

"Nowhere," Trace said, and put his hands on either side of her face. "You're staying right here. We've done nothing to be ashamed of."

"But I'm a mess," she argued. "Look at my hair." The last person she wanted to see was Philip. She always felt more vulnerable after she'd made love with Trace, and tonight was no exception.

He kissed her. "You look beautiful. We've taken care of your brother's objections to our relationship tonight. After Kevin, Philip will seem like a piece of cake."

Talia couldn't disagree more, but when Trace looked at her like that, she wouldn't refuse him anything. "Well, at least let me rinse off my face. I'll be back in a minute."

She turned to leave.

"Talia."

She looked back at him.

"Trace," Philip called from outside.

"Just one more minute, Philip," Trace answered, keeping his gaze fixed on Talia. "You know I love you, don't you?"

Her heart stopped, then beat out an unsteady rhythm. She stood still as a statue.

His grin held a touch of self-deprecation. "My timing's rotten, but I wanted you to know. I gotta let Philip in." He moved closer and gave her a hard, quick kiss. "We'll talk later."

*We'll talk later,* she repeated silently as she headed for the bathroom. That was only if she could ever speak again. It wasn't until she'd splashed her face with cold water that she realized what else Trace had said to her. A warm glow suffused her from her head to her toes.

In the mirror, she saw hair wild from Trace's fingers and a chin made pink by the rub of his five o'clock shadow. She also saw the special light in her eyes that he had put there. And the silly smile. He was responsible for that too. But deeper, in a place no one could see, she found herself hoping for forever, for the first time in her life.

Moments later she tentatively made her way to the foyer.

"I drove over to your new house," Philip was saying. "It looks real nice. Your housekeeper told me you'd gone to Gus's bar." He laughed. "I didn't believe her, but stopped by there anyway. They said you'd already left. I came in the back way to the house and spotted your 'Vette, so I stopped by."

Talia stepped into view then, and Philip stared at her. Trace reached for her and pulled her under his arm.

"You remember Talia, don't you?" Trace asked.

Philip's gaze took in her tousled appearance and the light seemed to dawn. "Yeah, I remember Talia," he said without enthusiasm. He shifted his fine leather shoes and crunched something beneath his foot. Leaning down, he picked up the small object. After studying it, he handed it to Talia.

"I believe this belongs to you." He gazed meaningfully at the gap on her white cotton shirt. "Looks like you've been busy," he went on, "but then, the McKenzies move fast. Hope I didn't interrupt anything."

Talia squeezed the button in her hand, mortified that Philip should be privy to the intimacies between her and Trace. It was obvious they'd been in a rush. She didn't mind that. What she minded was Philip's tone of voice and the way he looked at her as if she belonged on the bottom of his shoe.

Trace felt her stiffen and moved to correct Philip's impression. "Actually, I'm the one who's been rushing Talia. She wouldn't have anything to do with me in the beginning."

Philip looked at Trace as if Trace had lost his mind. "Hey, well, everyone needs a fling now and then—"

This time Trace stiffened. "This isn't a fling, Philip. I want Talia to marry me."

Talia stared at him.

Philip fought to compose himself. "But she's not . . ." He groped for the words.

Trace didn't even want to hear it. He especially didn't want Talia to hear it. He'd worked too hard to make her see how right they were for each other to have Philip mess it up now. He was beginning to think he'd made a mistake confronting Philip in front of her.

"I know exactly what you mean," he said, intentionally misinterpreting Philip. "She's not artificial. Talia doesn't love me for the Barringer name. She loves me for the man I am." Trace knew he was taking liberties, because she had never said she loved him. Not out loud anyway.

"She's perfect for me," he added, and squeezed her shoulder. He noticed Talia was having trouble keeping her jaw from going slack.

"Perfect?" Philip echoed.

"Yes, perfect," Trace said in his firmest CEO voice. "It's been great seeing you." He released Talia and went to the door. "You'll have to drop by the house tomorrow. There's something we need to discuss."

"Hell, no," Philip said in a rare display of temper. "I can't let you do something crazy like this, Trace. You've got to remember your position, your background. Talia's not—"

"Be careful, Philip," Trace interrupted in a low voice.

Talia's stomach churned at the tension between the two brothers. She should have insisted on leaving. Now all she could do was wait it out. Philip's insinuations had cast a tawdry light on something she'd believed was beautiful.

"I've always been careful," Philip said, then changed his tone. "Listen, Talia's attractive. She's probably great. But you don't want your whole life messed up just because of what she gives you between the sheets."

In one swift move, Trace slammed Philip against the wall. "I told you to be careful."

But the loss of Trace's control made Philip shed his. "She's a cheap slut who wants your money, you fool."

Trace drew back his fist, ready to strike.

Talia cried out. "Stop it. For God's sake, stop it. You're brothers."

Her voice penetrated the haze of Trace's fury. He took a deep breath and eased his hands away from Philip.

Philip eyed him warily and smoothed the wrinkles from his jacket. He cleared his throat. "I'll just try to forget this happened."

Talia saw the harshness in Trace's eyes. She felt a surge of foreboding and instinctively tried to prevent further damage. "That's probably a good idea," she said softly. "I'd like to go home, Trace."

"In a minute," he said, and her hopes fled.

"You know, Philip," he went on, "I've never noticed this snobbishness before. Either I've been blind, or you've hidden it well." He rubbed his face, and Talia could see the struggle going on inside him. "It raises other questions. And I want answers.

"Did you frame Kevin McKenzie?"

"No!" Philip's voice was loud, but Talia noticed he wouldn't look at Trace. "Is that what your little Talia told you?" he asked nastily.

Trace ignored that. "If you're lying to me," he said coldly, "Barringer Corporation will rescind its pledge for contributions to your political campaign."

Philip's Adam's apple bobbed. "I'm not lying. Dad will back me up," he added, and stomped out.

Talia could barely contain her disgust. There was about as much chance that Philip Barringer would tell the truth as there was that she and Trace would get married. A sense of the inevitable filled her, and her newborn hope withered and died.

Because she insisted, Trace took her home. He wanted to talk. She didn't. The atmosphere was fraught with an entirely different kind of tension than during the previous ride.

"He's sticking to his original story," Trace said.

"Do you believe him?"

He was silent for a moment, jamming the shift into third. Talia wondered if he was always this rough on his transmission.

"No," he finally said with a pain that came from his soul. "It's hard to accept that Philip, *my brother*, would do something like this, but I know he did. I'll never trust him again." He hesitated, then whispered, "It feels almost like he died."

With that statement, Talia realized what she'd been avoiding for weeks. The tie between Philip and Trace was just as strong as the tie between her and Kevin. The bond went back to childhood, strengthened by years and tears and laughter together.

The cord between siblings could be severed only through a deep, painful cut. The kind of cut that left scars and forever changed lives, perhaps destroying them.

She shook her head. She couldn't let that happen to Trace. It would make him bitter and suspicious. And even if Philip's deceit didn't stand between them, there was always, always, always the fact that Trace had more money in his back pocket than she had in her savings account.

She realized the rest of Trace's wealthy friends would echo Philip's sentiments—that she was after Trace's money. Although she considered herself a strong person, she didn't think she could happily spend the rest of her life battling those kind of innuendoes.

The lump in her throat swelled as tears threatened. She jerked back her composure, ignoring the pain. Her heart actually hurt.

"This doesn't change anything between us, Talia. We still belong together." His voice was solid, reassuring.

She took a deep breath. They were only a mile from her house. Quicker would be better. Trace had deep feelings for her, but he'd get over her. Another sharp pain hit, but she tossed it off.

"We don't belong together, Trace. It's been fun, but seeing Philip tonight took the kick out of it for me."

He turned to her in shock, then looked back at the road. "You're crazy."

"Maybe so," she said, stiffening her spine. "But don't call me anymore, Trace. Kevin's home now, and it would just make him uncomfortable. He's too important to me."

"I'm important to you," he said quietly. "Robby's important to you too."

The thought of Robby was one more lash from a whip. She'd grown to love the little boy. She closed her eyes and steeled herself. She was almost home.

"Not important enough," she said, throwing the knife and flinching inwardly as if she'd stabbed herself.

Trace stopped in front of her house and turned to her, his face set in hard lines. The confusion in his beautiful eyes nearly undid her.

"Dammit, Talia, you love me," he said harshly.

She almost admitted it. The feeling was so strong, it almost found its way to her lips. But her throat was getting tight again and her eyes were stinging. Crying wouldn't help her case.

"No," she said. "I don't."

# Ten

Talia held her breath until she reached her bedroom, then let it out, waiting for the tears. They never came.

A full ten minutes passed and an eerie tranquillity settled over her, like the calm before the storm. She'd expected pain without equal. Instead she just felt numb.

Yet she couldn't sit still. Rising from her bed, she began to pace. With odd detachment, she remembered the expression on Trace's face. First shock and then pain had tightened his mouth, and she had watched as every good feeling for her drained from him. She'd watched his eyes go flat and cold, and she shivered at the memory.

It had been important to watch, though, to seal the memory in her psyche. In the coming days when she felt weak and needy, she'd remember watching Trace's love die right in front of her. That way she wouldn't give in to foolish hopes and dreams.

The restlessness turned to fidgeting. She laced and unlaced her fingers. When she realized what she was doing, she cursed. She wouldn't be able to sleep, and if she kept this up, she'd wake Kevin and David.

Suddenly the room felt too small for her disquiet. The whole house felt too small. She put on a pair of tennis shoes and quietly left the house.

Although she didn't fear for her safety, one o'clock in the morning wasn't the best time for a jog. She ran anyway and thought of life before Trace. Her life had revolved around the shop and Kevin and a few friends. It would be that way again, she told herself.

A light rain began to fall. Still she ran, because she was still thinking of Trace and how he'd made her feel.

One foot after another pounded the black pavement. The monotonous pace soothed her restlessness, but it left her mind free to wander.

An ache started. At first she thought it was a stitch. When she pressed her pained side, however, it didn't wane. An image of Trace gently teasing her with words and caresses formed. The pain intensified.

She tried to think of something else, but her mind would not yield. It threw at her the memory of Robby cuddled against her, needing her. Was that a tear or a raindrop on her cheek?

The mental picture shifted to Trace again, in the jewelry shop, so eager to please.

The pain finally hit and Talia gasped at the force of it.

Images came faster and faster. Robby, his face covered with lime sherbet. Trace, eyes filled with laughter. Her pace slackened.

She could hear his voice. Her body jerked in response.

His scent was in her blood. *But you sent him away,* her heart accused.

She stopped and swayed, wondering if she'd made the biggest mistake in her life.

Pain struck her again and again, like a beating that would never end. Unable to withstand the blows, she doubled over and gave an anguished cry. With every cold word she'd flung to drive him away, she'd twisted the knife in her own heart.

A sob escaped, then another. And there on the dark street, she sat and wept her wounded heart out.

The next day Talia pinned a smile on her face and wished David a safe return to Massachusetts. But a whole tube of cover-up wouldn't conceal from her dear brother the ravages of her emotional upheaval.

Kevin hounded her relentlessly. He even followed her to the shop, asking prying questions while she did inventory. All this after she had been afraid he would be too hurt to speak to her.

"I don't want to talk about it," she said for the seventeenth time, and continued counting boxes of paper plates.

"That's too damn bad!" Kevin yelled. "You look like the bride of Frankenstein."

"Where did you get that silver tongue, brother mine?" she asked sweetly.

"Probably from the same family that gave you red eyes and a pink nose."

She jerked her head up and glared at him.

He sighed. "Red eyes and pink noses are fine for bunnies. But I don't like seeing them on my sister."

Her heart, what was left of it, softened. She touched his arm. "I'll be okay."

"Tell me," he said earnestly. "What did he do to you?"

She thought for a moment of all the things Trace

had done to her that had made her smile. Her eyes welled with moisture. Oh, Lord, not again, she thought. Between the night before and that morning she'd cried enough to fill a bathtub. She blinked rapidly, but a tear still escaped.

"I really, really don't want to talk about this," she whispered.

Kevin's face grew troubled. He caught her tear with a finger. "I really think we need to, especially if you've stopped seeing Trace because of me."

She sucked in a quick breath. She'd been waiting for this. "You were very angry last night."

He nodded, dropping his hand. "Mostly because I'd been left in the dark. I thought we were closer than that."

She closed her eyes against the guilt that ran through her. Setting her clipboard on a box, she tried to make him understand. "I'm sorry, Kevin, but it all seemed so unreal." She shook her head in wonder. "Who would have ever thought Trace Barringer and I would get together?"

"Not me," he muttered.

"See. It was pure insanity." And pure happiness. She shook that thought off. "I decided to wait until it all blew over to tell you. I mean, it couldn't last." She was reminding herself as much as him. "And I knew you'd rather see me date anyone besides Trace Barringer."

Kevin shifted. "Well, not anyone." He shoved his hands in the pockets of his jeans and looked away. A long moment passed. "He's not like Philip."

Talia recognized that as a huge concession. "You're right. He's not like Philip. As a matter of fact, Trace can be just as ruthlessly blunt as you can."

"Oh, yeah?" Kevin raised his eyebrows, then gave a knowing half smile. "I can see that after talking with him last night. He didn't waste any words about his feelings. He flat out said he loved you and wanted you."

Talia's heart squeezed into her throat. "That was before Phil—" She broke off abruptly, damning herself for opening her big mouth.

Kevin's eyes narrowed. "Before Philip what? Come on, Talia, what did he do? If he hurt you, I swear I'll beat the—"

"—you'll have to get in line," she interjected. "Philip showed up at Trace's last night. He said some . . . " She took a deep breath. " . . . some insulting things. Everything got out of hand and Trace shoved him against the wall. He was ready to hit him."

Kevin relaxed marginally. "My opinion of Trace is improving all the time."

She snatched up the clipboard. "That's nice, but I won't be seeing him anymore."

"Why not?"

Her anger and frustration suddenly peaked. She banged the clipboard down again and swung around to face him. "Because it won't work! Because Trace is rich and I'm not. Because Trace is well educated and I'm not. Because Trace will always be caviar and champagne and I'll always be subs and beer."

When she finished, she felt raw and out of breath. "It just won't work," she repeated in a broken voice.

Kevin stretched out his arms to enfold her, but she shook her head. "If you hug me, I'll cry again, and I'm tired of crying."

He stepped closer and managed to ruffle her hair and keep his distance at the same time. "It's your decision, big sister, but I've got a gut feeling Trace Barringer won't be easy to shake."

After last night, Talia thought, shaking Trace should be very easy. "I'll worry about that if it happens." She gathered her injured feelings together and mentally stuffed them deep inside her. "Right now I'm going to finish my inventory."

Kevin watched her for a few moments while she counted napkins. "You ever hear of Cinderella?"

"Yes," she said in a crisp voice. "It's a fairy tale."

After that she buried herself in work. Throughout the day she caught Kevin's worried glances when he didn't think she was looking. He seemed to understand her need to stay busy and didn't question her. What he did do, in her opinion, was much worse.

He was nice to her.

He fixed dinner every night, helped her at the shop, and gave her lots of hugs. Under his affection and care, she found it increasingly difficult not to burst into tears. Especially when he fielded Trace's telephone calls.

She couldn't believe Trace was actually calling her, even after what she'd said, what she'd done. And she had done the right thing. Hadn't she? She knew she'd acted impulsively out of hurt and fear. Was that wise?

She felt cruel for denying her love to Trace. He'd been so generous about his feelings with her. Was that fair?

Questions and doubts constantly assailed her. Had she been wrong? When she thought about it, she realized that there were always obstacles to love. Problems always crept up. Still, people managed to work them out.

That thought burrowed its way deep into her heart and mind as the day for the LAM auction drew closer.

Trace was immersed in his own problems. On the business front, he'd had to institute a hiring freeze his foremen weren't happy about. After allowing them to whine for a few minutes, he'd offered the alternatives of decreasing pay or layoffs. The whining had abruptly ceased.

His personal life was shot to hell. Robby had the chicken pox. He was fussy and uncomfortable. He asked for candy, Reptiles, and Talia. Trace provided the first two and sighed over the last. *Join the crowd, kid,* he told his son silently. *I want her too.*

When Talia had rejected him, he'd been stunned into silence. She'd brought him love and tenderness. When he was with her, he could be himself. His name and position meant nothing to her. Being with her, basking in her attention and love, was like finding a home he'd only dreamed of. Now she was gone.

Anger and hurt rumbled inside him, robbing him of sleep and sense. He'd repeatedly called her, only to end up speaking to her stonewalling brother. Unwilling to accept her rejection, he took action. He put more pressure on Philip and discussed Kevin McKenzie with his father. Harlan closed up like a clam, but Trace thought he saw uncertainty in his father's eyes. Or perhaps it was guilt.

Friday morning the day before the LAM auction, Philip strolled into his office bright and early. "How's Robby?" he asked, sliding into a leather chair.

"Itchy." Looking at his brother, Trace remembered when Talia had sat in that chair. He adjusted his glasses. His eyes were dry and sensitive from lack of sleep, and wearing his contact lenses was like putting a cactus in his eye.

"I have this idea about the charity auction tomorrow," Philip announced after skimming the pleasantries.

Trace was filled with a lethal determination to hear

the truth from Philip. He'd give his brother three minutes. "I didn't know you were coming."

"I wouldn't miss it. The press will be there in droves." He paused for a second. "I want to announce my intention to run for state senate."

Trace didn't respond. The tension in the room raised a notch.

"I want an endorsement from Barringer Corporation."

"I haven't gotten all my answers yet."

Philip's face tightened. "You've talked to Dad."

Trace nodded. "I talked. He didn't. I've got a call in to Valerie, but her housekeeper says she's in France. The only thing I've learned is something about Kevin's lawyer. Funny thing. He left town right after Kevin was sent to the detention center. You wouldn't know anything about it would you?"

Philip shook his head.

Trace leaned forward across his desk. "It's time to quit running from the issue, Philip. It's time for the truth."

Philip stood and whirled away, not looking at him.

"She's pushing you to do this, isn't she? It's Talia McKenzie." He shook his head. "It's a sad day when a Barringer turns against his brother."

Trace waved his hand. "Save the Barringer propaganda for Dad. I'm not turning against you. I just want the truth."

"I've told you—"

"Nothing," Trace cut in, his patience gone. "And that's what you're going to get from Barringer Corporation."

Philip set his jaw. He crossed the office to the window and stood there, looking out. He was silent for so long, Trace was certain he'd never tell him. Then Philip spoke.

"Kevin McKenzie and Valerie were sneaking around together. It was right after Dad's first heart attack. You were in law school." His voice was toneless. "I warned Kevin to stop seeing Valerie. He didn't, so I handled it."

"You handled it!" Trace's fury hit him like a tidal wave. He jumped up and stalked over to Philip. "You handled it by framing an innocent boy, by having him institutionalized in a place that robbed him of his youth. In a place where he got stabbed." Trace jerked his brother around to face him. "What gave you the right to play God with Kevin McKenzie's life?"

Philip gazed blankly at him.

"I'm a Barringer. We look out for each other."

Trace was floored by such twisted reasoning. "Not that way! Never that way. Do you realize you could be disbarred for this?"

Philip shook his head. "Who'll ever know? Besides, I was only twenty."

The bitter taste of disgust filled Trace's mouth. "You make me sick. I don't know you anymore. Maybe I never did. You've lost your ethics and your integrity. You don't feel an ounce of regret for nearly ruining someone's life." He ran his fingers through his hair. "Where's the guy who decided when he was twelve that he wanted to be a lawyer, so he could fight for justice and fairness for everyone? Where's the guy who marched on Washington to protest for something he believed in? Where, for God's sake," Trace asked, flinging out a hand to encompass the room, "is my brother Philip?"

Seconds ticked by, the silence stretching between them swollen with disappointment and anger. Philip looked shaken. "I don't know." He cleared his throat and looked away from Trace. "Maybe I'd better find out."

There was nothing else Trace could say. His sense of betrayal was too great for words. The room couldn't contain his disapproval. He felt it with every breath he took. Unable to bear the sight of his brother, he turned away.

Another silence passed until Trace heard the muted sound of Philip's footsteps on the carpet, a pause, then the opening and closing of the door.

Trace sighed and removed his glasses. The disillusionment was crushing. To know that Philip had been so destructive and deceitful wounded Trace. Yet at the same time, he felt as if someone had lifted a weight from his chest. He no longer felt a war of his loyalties. He understood Talia's pain and wanted to help her with it. One more barrier between him and her had been removed. Still, he wondered if it would make any difference to her, or if it was just too late.

The auction was held in the lush gardens of the Hidden Hills Country Club. Azaleas and roses bloomed in profusion as guests wandered from the tables filled with the merchandise to chairs beneath a canopy. Uniformed waiters served mimosas and pastries. The Fitzgerald sisters had created an atmosphere of sociable relaxation.

Talia, however, was ready to tear her hair out. She'd hoped to see Trace before the auction began. She'd carefully chosen a peach floral dress that swayed and swirled when she moved. It was the most feminine dress she'd ever owned. It was also off the rack, but she didn't think Trace would mind.

If he would just get there. She'd rehearsed her plan. She would ask him to meet privately with her after the auction. It would all be very civilized. When they were alone, she would apologize and confess her love, and pray that he would take her back.

Her nervous pacing was interrupted by Martha Fitzgerald's amplified voice. She welcomed everyone and gave recognition to a few special donations, then the auctioneer took over.

Talia didn't sit. She stood to the side craning her neck for a first glance of Trace. At last she saw him walking swiftly along the outer edge of the garden. Her heart rose to her throat and her feet moved of their own accord, first walking, then running.

In the background, she heard the auctioneer say, "The first item up for bid is a Ming vase donated by Camilia Wentworth . . . "

As she raced toward Trace, Talia drank in the sight of him. His hair was mussed, he wore his tinted glasses, and his mouth was set in a forbidding straight line.

He looked ready for a fight.

"Let's open the bidding at two thousand . . ."

After almost losing a sandal in her mad dash, she suddenly found herself standing in front of Trace. Her mind went blank.

She couldn't see his eyes. Lord, she'd give up Chinese food for a year just to see his eyes. She opened her mouth at the same time he did.

"Trace, I'm so—"

"Talia, I talked to—"

They both fell silent. Talia took a deep breath and watched Trace take one too. Perhaps that was a good sign. Still, she prayed she'd find the right words. He deserved an apology and the truth about her feelings, even if he'd changed his mind himself. Civilized or not, she felt compelled to tell him now rather than after the auction.

She cleared her throat. "I'm sorry. I was wrong. I do—"

He shook his head, and her heart plummeted. "No," he said. "I talked to Philip and found out the truth."

Her feeling of desperation heightened. "It doesn't mat—"

He covered her lips with his fingers. "Yes, it does." He took her arm and pulled her away from the crowd. "I should have believed you, but it was hard to accept that Philip could be so vicious."

His voice was low and tense, and she could imagine the struggle he'd gone through. She clenched her hands together.

"He finally admitted it, but even now, I'm not sure if he feels any regret." He raked a hand through his hair and looked away. "After he told me, I felt this horrible shame, because he didn't seem to have the sense to feel it for himself. When I think of what this has cost you and Kevin, I wonder if there was anything I could have done to prevent it."

"Oh, no," she whispered. Everything within her protested the pain in his voice. She reached for his arm. "You must *never ever* blame yourself for this. You had nothing to do with it." She searched his face. "I can't stand to see you torn between Philip and me. That's why I told you I wouldn't see you again."

His reaction was swift. He captured her hand in his and said, "I'm not torn."

The near-violent intensity behind his words shook her. "I'm not either. That's what I was trying to tell you. The stuff about Kevin and Philip isn't important. The fact that you have more money than I ever will isn't important either. None of that is as important as you are." Her voice broke. "As we are together."

"Ah, Talia." He pulled her into his arms. "I thought I'd lost you. Do you know what you put me through? I was ready to kidnap you to get you back."

"I've been miserable," she confessed. "You're all I've thought about." She remembered the endless hours she'd spent arguing with herself. "At first I tried to tell myself ending it was for the best, but my heart refused to believe it. Even Kevin didn't believe it."

"Kevin?"

She let out a nervous little laugh. "Yes, Kevin. I don't know what you said to him, but he told me you wouldn't be easy to shake."

"He was damn right about that," Trace muttered roughly.

"That and a few other things. It took me a while, but I finally realized that everyone has problems." She looked into his face, wishing once again she could see his eyes. "People who really care about each other solve their problems together. But I want you to know—"

"*Together*," he cut in. "I won't let you go again, Talia. It would be easier to cut off my arm. You belong to me." He pressed his mouth to hers in a firm, utterly possessive kiss. "If you have any doubts, we'll take care of them once we're married. And we *are* getting married as soon as possible." He spoke as if he were offering a nonnegotiable contract.

Relief made her giddy, but she remembered there was one more thing she needed to tell him. "Trace," she began.

"I mean it. I'm not taking no for an answer."

"Trace."

"You can just get used to the idea. I'm not letting you out of my sight or my bed."

Her heart soared. It was incredible to hear him say these things, but she was having a hard time getting a word in edgewise.

"Trace," she said, fighting for breath and a measure of sanity after another hard kiss. "Shut up and take off your glasses."

His brief hesitation revealed he was more accustomed to giving orders than receiving them. He complied nonetheless. His eyes were bloodshot but determined. His jaw was clenched.

That she'd made him suffer grieved her unbearably.

She touched his cheek and kissed it. "I wanted to see your eyes," she said softly, "when I told you that I love you."

A spark flickered to life in those green eyes.

"You are the most wonderful man," she went on, her own eyes filling with tears. "Sometimes I have a hard time believing that you could really truly love me."

"I couldn't love anyone else." He brought her closer still and lowered his mouth until it was a breath from hers. "Will you marry me?"

"Whenever you say," she promised, staring into a face she would cherish the rest of her days.

"Sold!" the auctioneer shouted as they sealed their promise with a kiss.

# *Epilogue*

One week later, Talia's dress was not only off the rack, it was on the floor, along with her bra and panties, and her husband's shirt, trousers, and briefs. The blue Caribbean beckoned below the open window of their honeymoon suite. A palm tree rustled in the warm breeze.

The ice in the champagne bucket had long since melted. The white satin coverlet lay on the floor, too, and Talia Barringer had the best arms this side of heaven wrapped around her.

Trace toyed with her hair. "You're not talking."

She smiled. "I'm counting my blessings."

He nuzzled her cheek. "You are?"

"Yes. There's Robby."

He kissed her nose in agreement.

"And there's the fact that Kevin has accepted our relationship. He even seems to respect you." Her smile wavered. "I wish I could say the same for Philip."

Trace snuggled her closer and ran a soothing hand down her arm. "He's not running for election anymore. Maybe he'll take the time to find himself again. That would be a blessing."

"That's true." Because she didn't want to focus on any unpleasantness, she went on counting. "But the best blessing of all," she said, laying her hand over his heart, "is you."

He shook his head. "No. It's you."

She shook her head, too, her grin widening. Before she could open her mouth, however, Trace covered it with his. With a soft sigh and a full heart, she decided she could continue this loving argument for the rest of her life.

# THE EDITOR'S CORNER

Next month's lineup sizzles with BAD BOYS, heroes who are too hot to handle but too sinful to resist. In six marvelous romances, you'll be held spellbound by these men's deliciously wicked ways and daring promises of passion. Whether they're high-powered attorneys, brash jet jockeys, or modern-day pirates, BAD BOYS are masters of seduction who never settle for anything less than what they want. And the heroines learn that surrender comes all too easily when the loving is all too good. . . .

Fighter pilot Devlin MacKenzie in **MIDNIGHT STORM** by Laura Taylor, LOVESWEPT #576, is the first of our BAD BOYS. He and David Winslow, the hero of DESERT ROSE, LOVESWEPT #555, flew together on a mission that ended in a horrible crash, and now Devlin has come to Jessica Cleary's inn to recuperate. She broke their engagement years before, afraid to love a man who lives dangerously, but the rugged warrior changes her mind in a scorchingly sensual courtship. Laura turns up the heat in this riveting romance.

**SHAMELESS**, LOVESWEPT #577, by Glenna McReynolds, is the way Colt Haines broke Sarah Brooks's heart by leaving town without a word after the night she'd joyfully given him her innocence. Ten years later a tragedy brings him back to Rock Creek, Wyoming. He vows not to stay, but with one look at the woman she's become, he's determined to make her understand why he'd gone—and to finally make her his. Ablaze with the intensity of Glenna's writing, **SHAMELESS** is a captivating love story.

Cutter Beaumont *is* an **ISLAND ROGUE**, LOVESWEPT #578, by Charlotte Hughes, and he's also the mayor, sheriff, and owner of the Last Chance Saloon. Ellie Parks isn't interested though. She's come to the South Carolina island looking for a peaceful place to silence the demons that haunt her dreams—and instead she finds a handsome rake who wants to keep her up nights. Charlotte masterfully resolves this trouble in paradise with a series of events that will make you laugh and cry.

Jake Madison is nothing but **BAD COMPANY** for Nila Shepherd in Theresa Gladden's new LOVESWEPT, #579. When his sensual gaze spots her across the casino, Jake knows he must possess the temptress in the come-and-get-me dress. Nila has always wanted to walk on the wild side, but the fierce desire Jake awakens in her has her running for cover. Still, there's no hiding from this man who makes it his mission to fulfill her fantasies. Theresa just keeps coming up with terrific romances, and aren't we lucky?

Our next LOVESWEPT, #580 by Olivia Rupprecht, has one of the best titles ever—**HURTS SO GOOD**. And legendary musician Neil Grey certainly knows about hurting; that's why he dropped out of the rat race and now plays only in his New Orleans bar. Journalist Andrea Post would try just about anything to uncover his mystery, to write the story no one ever had, but the moment he calls her *"chère,"* he steals her heart. Another memorable winner from Olivia!

Suzanne Forster's stunning contribution to the BAD BOYS month is **NIGHT OF THE PANTHER**, LOVESWEPT #581. Johnny Starhawk is a celebrated lawyer whose killer instincts and Irish-Apache heritage have made him a star, but he's never forgotten the woman who'd betrayed him. And now, when Honor Bartholomew is forced to seek his help, will he give in to his need for revenge . . . or his love for the only woman he's ever wanted? This romance of smoldering anger and dangerous desire is a tour de force from Suzanne.

On sale this month from FANFARE are four terrific novels. **DIVINE EVIL** is the most chilling romantic suspense novel yet from best-selling author Nora Roberts. When successful sculptor Clare Kimball returns to her hometown, she discovers that there's a high price to pay for digging up the secrets of the past. But she finds an ally in the local sheriff, and together they confront an evil all the more terrifying because those who practice it believe it is divine.

**HAVING IT ALL** by critically acclaimed author Maeve Haran is a tender, funny, and revealing novel about a woman who does have it all—a glittering career, an exciting husband, and two adorable children. But she tires of pretending she's superwoman, and her search for a different kind of happiness and success shocks the family and friends she loves.

With **HIGHLAND FLAME**, Stephanie Bartlett brings back the beloved heroine of HIGHLAND REBEL. In this new novel, Catriona Galbraid and her husband, Ian, depart Scotland's Isle of Skye after they're victorious in their fight for justice for the crofters. But when a tragedy leaves Cat a widow, she's thrust into a new struggle—and into the arms of a new love.

Talented Virginia Lynn creates an entertaining variation on the taming-of-the-shrew theme with **LYON'S PRIZE**. In medieval England the Saxon beauty Brenna of Marwald is forced to marry Rye de Lyon, the Norman knight known as the Black Lion. She vows that he will never have her love, but he captures her heart with passion.

Sharon and Tom Curtis are among the most talented authors of romantic fiction, and you wouldn't want to miss this chance to pick up a copy of their novel **THE GOLDEN TOUCH**, which LaVyrle Spencer has praised as being "pure pleasure!" This beautifully written romance has two worlds colliding when an internationally famous pop idol moves into the life of a small-town teacher.

The Delaneys are coming! Once again Kay Hooper, Iris Johansen, and Fayrene Preston have collaborated to bring you a sparkling addition to this remarkable family's saga. Look for **THE DELANEY CHRISTMAS CAROL**—available soon from FANFARE.

Happy reading!

With best wishes,

Nita Taublib
Associate Publisher
LOVESWEPT and FANFARE

## OFFICIAL RULES TO WINNERS CLASSIC SWEEPSTAKES

No Purchase necessary. To enter the sweepstakes follow instructions found elsewhere in this offer. You can also enter the sweepstakes by hand printing your name, address, city, state and zip code on a 3" x 5" piece of paper and mailing it to: Winners Classic Sweepstakes, P.O. Box 785, Gibbstown, NJ 08027. Mail each entry separately. Sweepstakes begins 12/1/91. Entries must be received by 6/1/93. Some presentations of this sweepstakes may feature a deadline for the Early Bird prize. If the offer you receive does, then to be eligible for the Early Bird prize your entry must be received according to the Early Bird date specified. Not responsible for lost, late, damaged, misdirected, illegible or postage due mail. Mechanically reproduced entries are not eligible. All entries become property of the sponsor and will not be returned.

Prize Selection/Validations: Winners will be selected in random drawings on or about 7/30/93, by VENTURA ASSOCIATES, INC., an independent judging organization whose decisions are final. Odds of winning are determined by total number of entries received. Circulation of this sweepstakes is estimated not to exceed 200 million. Entrants need not be present to win. All prizes are guaranteed to be awarded and delivered to winners. Winners will be notified by mail and may be required to complete an affidavit of eligibility and release of liability which must be returned within 14 days of date of notification or alternate winners will be selected. Any guest of a trip winner will also be required to execute a release of liability. Any prize notification letter or any prize returned to a participating sponsor, Bantam Doubleday Dell Publishing Group, Inc., its participating divisions or subsidiaries, or VENTURA ASSOCIATES, INC. as undeliverable will be awarded to an alternate winner. Prizes are not transferable. No multiple prize winners except as may be necessary due to unavailability, in which case a prize of equal or greater value will be awarded. Prizes will be awarded approximately 90 days after the drawing. All taxes, automobile license and registration fees, if applicable, are the sole responsibility of the winners. Entry constitutes permission (except where prohibited) to use winners' names and likenesses for publicity purposes without further or other compensation.

Participation: This sweepstakes is open to residents of the United States and Canada, except for the province of Quebec. This sweepstakes is sponsored by Bantam Doubleday Dell Publishing Group, Inc. (BDD), 666 Fifth Avenue, New York, NY 10103. Versions of this sweepstakes with different graphics will be offered in conjunction with various solicitations or promotions by different subsidiaries and divisions of BDD. Employees and their families of BDD, its division, subsidiaries, advertising agencies, and VENTURA ASSOCIATES, INC., are not eligible.

Canadian residents, in order to win, must first correctly answer a time limited arithmetical skill testing question. Void in Quebec and wherever prohibited or restricted by law. Subject to all federal, state, local and provincial laws and regulations.

Prizes: The following values for prizes are determined by the manufacturers' suggested retail prices or by what these items are currently known to be selling for at the time this offer was published. Approximate retail values include handling and delivery of prizes. Estimated maximum retail value of prizes: 1 Grand Prize ($27,500 if merchandise or $25,000 Cash); 1 First Prize ($3,000); 5 Second Prizes ($400 each); 35 Third Prizes ($100 each); 1,000 Fourth Prizes ($9.00 each) ; 1 Early Bird Prize ($5,000); Total approximate maximum retail value is $50,000. Winners will have the option of selecting any prize offered at level won. Automobile winner must have a valid driver's license at the time the car is awarded. Trips are subject to space and departure availability. Certain black-out dates may apply. Travel must be completed within one year from the time the prize is awarded. Minors must be accompanied by an adult. Prizes won by minors will be awarded in the name of parent or legal guardian.

For a list of Major Prize Winners (available after 7/30/93): send a self-addressed, stamped envelope entirely separate from your entry to: Winners Classic Sweepstakes Winners, P.O. Box 825, Gibbstown, NJ 08027. Requests must be received by 6/1/93. DO NOT SEND ANY OTHER CORRESPONDENCE TO THIS P.O. BOX.